I0517001

VALKYRIE

Tales of the Asgard

Book 1

ANITA COX

Copyright © 2016 Anita Cox
All rights reserved. by Syn Publishing, LLC., 2016.
No part of this novel may be copied, reproduced, photocopied,
or transmitted in any form or by any electronic, mechanical,
recording, or retrieval system, nor by any other means, including
recording or by any information storage and retrieval systems,
without written permission of the publisher or author, except as
permitted under the U.S. Copyright Act of 1976.
This is a work of fiction. Names, characters, places, and
incidents are the production of the author's imagination or are
used fictitiously. Any resemblance to actual persons, living or
dead, events, or locales is entirely and completely coincidental.
The name "Syn Publishing" and its logo are trademarks of Syn
Publishing LLC.,
Printed in the United States of America.
Visit us on line at www.SynPublishing.com.

ISBN: 1-942632-21-5
ISBN-13: 978-1-942632-21-4

DEDICATION

To my loyal and wonderful fans. You are the reason I keep doing this crazy thing. From the reviews to the messages asking for more, I truly thank you.

To Ella Dominguez and Crystal Solis, my girls! Thank you for your continued friendship and support. I don't think I could make it through some days without you holding me up!

And my McB's, who have stuck around with all of your naughtiness for the last five years. Your friendship, means the world to me. The crazy posts, fun little surprises in the mail, and support are second to none.

Most importantly, to family. Without you, the rest is meaningless..

CONTENTS

ACKNOWLEDGMENTS

Thank you to Coffee and Characters for your brutal edits.

CHAPTER ONE

There were many theories about how the world began. Was it a big bang? Did some magical creature in the sky work diligently for seven days and seven nights to create the Earth and the heavens? That didn't matter now, not now that the end had come.

Vallah had been born into a world without disease; a world where one could expect to live to at least 150 years old, thanks to a gift from an alien race known as the Centurions. One simple vaccine eradicated disease and infection. They bestowed gifts of technology upon the human race. The Centurions said they wanted nothing in return other than to assist the humans into advancing like other races of other planets. They wanted to bring the humans up to speed. That...was a lie.

A convenient side effect of longevity without illness was a lack of fertility. The ticking time bomb of the Centurion gift grew slowly, as fewer and fewer couples were able to conceive. Of those children born, over eighty percent of them were male, and that number was growing.

In a male-dominated world with very few fertile females, freedom had been stripped from the very mothers who brought them into this world. At the ripe age of eleven, young women would be tested. Those who had eggs were branded as breeders. Men could claim them, marry them, and force them to breed like livestock.

Less fortunate were the remaining women who were traded like property to those whose desires were perverse in nature. By the time a girl was fourteen, she'd be married off to whoever claimed her, giving parents one of two choices. They could try to find a suitable marriage, to the least disgusting choice. Or they could try to hide her.

Those who hid their children suffered greatly.

So did those who married their daughters off.

Vallah's mother was no ordinary human, and she wasn't about to risk hiding her underground or in the mountains. She dragged the eleven-year-old into the basement, both mother and child sobbing. Mother sorrowful, and daughter terrified.

With tear-filled eyes, Valerie kissed her sweet Vallah on the forehead and whispered something in a language Vallah didn't recognize. "I love you. You'll come back to me. You're going somewhere special with people I trust. They will train you to become a great warrior. I will say a prayer for you every day for the next ten years, Vallah, and pray that Odin keeps and protects you."

"Mom. Mom, where am I going?"

When her mother pulled a book off the shelf that slid the entire bookshelf to the side, revealing a hidden passage, she became frightened. While her mother professed her undying love for her daughter, she pushed Vallah so quickly down the hall the little girl stumbled. When they reached the end of the tunnel, her mother opened the door to a very small room made of stone. Inside was a glass box, which looked like a see-through casket standing on its end. A small brown leather bag rested at the entrance.

"Close your eyes, the light is very bright. When it dims, you can open them and you'll be far, far away from this madness." Her chest shuddered.

Vallah slung her arms around her mother's waist. "Don't make me leave! I don't want to go!"

Valerie sobbed briefly before taking a deep, cleansing breath, and then got on her knees. "Listen to me. Your life will be ugly, very ugly, if you remain here. You will be hurt all of the time. I cannot let that happen. I'm doing for you what my mother did for me, and her mother for her. It's what I will do for your baby sister if I have to. When you come back, you'll be strong. You can fight them off. I will have someone waiting here for you, I promise." After peeling Vallah off of her, she forced her in the box. "Close your eyes."

The white light blinded her, even with her eyes closed, before it dimmed again. When Vallah opened her eyes, three tall women stood, wearing clothing made of leather. Two wore pants and a halter top; one wore what looked like a skirt and a bra. Each had a deep bronze hue to their skin like Vallah had never seen. They almost seemed to shimmer.

"Come on out, Vallah. It's okay." The woman in the center extended her hand. Her mocha hair fell over her shoulder in a thick braid. Her emerald eyes softened as she looked down on the frightened adolescent. "I'm Nadia. I'll be your combat instructor. We've much to learn."

The moment she stepped out of the glass box, something inside her changed. Something died. Not only was the fear and loss gone from her heart, but so was everything else. What made her Vallah died that day in the glass casket. From that point forward, she was someone entirely different.

For ten years she was a quiet yet diligent student. She did as her masters asked, and studied harder than required. She learned various forms of close quarters combat skills from ancient stick fighting to Aikido, and became skilled with swords and knives of various sizes. They taught her to be stealthy, to sneak in, get the job done, and sneak out. Olivia her scholastic master, made her study every aspect

ANITA COX

of human history, math, psychology, and as much science as Vallah could wrap her head around.

She spent most nights alone, trying to remember the giddy little girl who played with her little sister, Faith, under the willow tree. She tried to remember Faith's laugh, their mother's warm embrace, and their father's bedtime stories.

By the time she reached adulthood, her education had changed. Tatiana, a redhead with a fiery temper and a penchant for recon, caught Vallah spying on her while receiving pleasure from a local villager. Instead of the beating Vallah thought was coming, she was invited to come in and watch up close…that was, until Tatiana gave her a man of her own for her nineteenth birthday.

The local, Seth, was a tall boy with light brown hair and ocean-blue eyes. He was patient and kind as Vallah explored sex for the first time. It was the first emotion Vallah had felt since stepping out of her casket and into the world of the Amazonians. The passion within her stirred each time she met with him.

Her first orgasm made her nearly insatiable. Her heart seemed to beat again as the fires burned deep within her. How could she get such pleasure from a man, when it was men and their greed that caused her to be sent away?

The anger-fueled passion ignited during Seth's visits.

One evening, Seth was exceptionally attentive. Vallah sat in his lap with her back facing him, her legs draped over his, leaving her wide and exposed. He kept two fingers swirling expertly over her swollen bud as he pushed into her from below. With his other hand he massaged her breasts, tweaking her nipples occasionally, driving her wild.

Her chestnut hair clung to her face as she gasped with every thrust. When he licked the side of her neck, ever so slightly, gooseflesh formed down her arm, giving her a shiver, and another sensation that only led to heighten her arousal. The pressure began to build low in her belly, and her muscles clenched as she fought to match each stroke

4

with one of her own. Her grip on the chair tightened.

He nibbled on her ear, whispering words in a foreign language she didn't recognize, but the sound was erotic. It led to her undoing. Her body tensed as a wave of euphoria washed over her. She released the air in her lungs as she moaned, riding the wave through the end. Seth stood, picking her up as he rose, and placed her on the bed.

"That was amazing," she cooed.

"You make it amazing. You're such an exquisite creature, Vallah. I'm going to miss you," he whispered. "I'm leaving tomorrow on a mission. I don't know when I will return."

"Mission? What sort of mission?" She pushed her hair from her face, which was still damp with perspiration.

"I've been told it's a rescue mission. That's all I know. But I do know it will take me far, far from here, and from you." He cupped her hand in his. "Do you love me?" His blue eyes searched hers for some hint of how she felt.

"I have no idea what that is, Seth. But I do look forward to seeing you." Did she really have a cold, dead heart? Was it really possible that the only thing she could feel was physical pleasure?

With a pained smile, he stroked her arm. "We'll see each other again. I just hope you recognize me."

She laughed and nudged toward him. "I think I'd recognize every inch of your body by now."

"But…what if my face changed? Like, what if I was scarred in battle?"

"Seriously?" She rolled her eyes. "Could you not speak?"

"What if you didn't believe it was I?" His smile faded. Seriousness set in.

"Okay, well, Tatiana always told me the best tool for those who wish to remain tied yet hidden was a secret code—a word that only those who are safe would know."

"Bella," he whispered in her ear. "That's the word. When I whisper it in your ear, you'll know it's me, even if

I've changed."

She stood from the bed, unwilling to play the game any longer. "You're nuts."

"Yes, I know. I'm nuts about you."

Cinching her robe closed, she rolled her eyes. "It's time for me to go. When you return from your mission, come see me."

"What if I'm not back before you return home?" His head hung low, along with his shoulders.

"That's a year from now, Seth. I'm sure you'll return before that. Now, I have to get back to my hut. I have to be up before the sun to learn a new technique from Tatiana, and she doesn't accept tardiness." She grabbed the handle to the door and turned to look at Seth one last time. "I'm not sure what love is. But I do care very deeply about you."

That was the last time they met. A year did, in fact, go by without his return. The sadness of his absence was replaced by her apprehension. It was time to go home.

She questioned whether or not she'd recognize her family. The vague images in her mind were but mere ghosts in her dreams, and had been for at least the last five years. Her masters stood before her to say goodbye.

Tatiana, with her blazing red hair, hugged her. "You're a fine warrior, Vallah. We will see each other again soon."

Nadia, the tallest of them and bronzed like a goddess, put her palms on Vallah's biceps. "You've learned all we have to teach. It's your time now. Go out in the world and make your mark. You have made me proud."

Katana, who'd mothered her most, stood in Nadia's image, only slightly shorter. "Show them what an Amazon warrior has to answer with. Let no man mistake you for weak. I've been honored to be your master and blessed to have you as a student."

While it may have seemed like a cold sendoff, this was more than emotional for her Amazon masters. She enjoyed their warm embrace one last time.

She stepped into the transporter with all of her belongings—mostly weapons—and closed her eyes. The blinding light washed over her, and then everything grew dark. Pushing her hands forward, she forced the door open. Her eyes were not adjusting to the severity of the darkness that surrounded her. *Did the transporter malfunction?*

After retrieving a light from her hip bag, she clicked it on. The only thing in the room was a cardboard box. Written on the side of the box was her name, *Vallah*. She pulled the lid open and found a small recorder and a stack of cash. After tucking the cash in her satchel, she grabbed up the recorder and pressed the power button. A hologram of her mother projected in front of her.

"Vallah, if you're seeing this, the chances are great that we didn't make it. The government has been raiding houses. They're angry that you're missing, that more and more fertile girls are disappearing." Her image looked at the floor briefly, then back up toward her. "Your sister has been married off in hopes of protecting her. You must find her. Find her and take her back to where I sent you. You're the last of our bloodline."

She paused the hologram and shone her flashlight around the room one more time. The door was sealed. When she resumed the hologram, her mother gave her the answer she needed. "Proceed to the wall adjacent to the transporter. Press the third brick from the left, eight rows from the ceiling. It'll reveal a safe passage. May Odin be with you."

That's it? No declaration of love? No "I missed you"? Nothing? She threw the device as hard as she could against the floor. It exploded into a thousand pieces. Her chest heaved as she cursed her family, the government, and the world.

She knew she could not stay in the dark room. There was no air there. Gathering herself, she trudged forward toward the wall. After finding the special brick, the wall moved, revealing a lit pathway. At the end of the path were five stairs that led to a door. The Amazons taught her to be fearless—to tackle each obstacle as it appeared. But something gave her pause. Her hand rested on the door, the world on the other side, but what of the world? What had it become? The Amazons were sheltered, living in an undisclosed location hidden on Earth. They had never told her where they were, only that they were confident no one would ever find them.

The world on the other side of the door was horrible, of this much she was certain. The transporter had removed the foreign ink from her arm—no one would know she could procreate. Still, women had been treated as property when she'd left. How bad had it become in the last decade?

With one cleansing breath, she pushed. The cool night breeze kissed her face and blew her dark locks back. It had been ten years, but she recognized the smell immediately as the woods that bordered her family's property. The door was concealed in the willow tree on the forest's edge, a tree she'd played in a thousand times before.

Where the house should have been, there was now a pile of rubble. The air escaped her lungs as she fell to her knees. It was all gone. The family photos, the china passed down from mother to daughter, her room. Everything. Were they all dead? Incarcerated?

Get up. Get up and move.

CHAPTER TWO

She didn't recall walking into town. She couldn't recall much until the barmaid snapped her fingers before her face. "Snap out of it, girl. What are you on?"

"She is in shock, I think," another voice called out.

"Uh, yeah, I came to visit my aunt, but their house has been decimated." She blinked rapidly, trying to gather her wits. "The Sigrids. Do you know what happened to them?"

The barmaid was a big woman, tall and hefty but not fat. She leaned in toward Vallah, resting on her elbows. "That happened about five years ago or so. After the breeder disappeared, they married the sister off to Mayor Snow. That's when things took a turn. Eventually, the sister spilled the family beans, said the mother hid the breeder. Both of the parents were black-bagged by McCray and his heathens. Questioned for weeks, I heard. No one has seen them since."

"Fuck," she choked out. "All that for hiding their kid?"

A man grabbed Vallah's arm, pushing up her sleeve. His large, meaty hook crushed her forearm. She fought the urge to slice his throat. Tatiana had stressed that while she was trained for immediate reaction, she needed a cool, calm head in public.

"I'm not a breeder. Fuck off." She pushed him away. *So much for cool and calm.*

His dark eyes narrowed. Yellow rotting teeth grinded behind his open mouth. The stench of tobacco and whiskey oozed out of him. "I can still claim you, little lady. It's my right."

"Can I get a shot first?" She forced a smile at him, though she had to ignore the bile in her throat. She'd have to get rid of the slimy bastard soon. The shot would buy her a few moments to form a plan on dealing with him.

"You're gonna need it." When he grinned, she received another flash of his yellowed smile. With all of the advancements in modern medicine, this man obviously couldn't manage simple hygiene. The thought of that putrefying face anywhere near her had her skin crawling.

The barmaid slid a glass to her filled with clear liquid. "Best I got. I made it a double," she said with a nod.

The liquid burned its way down her throat and warmed her belly when it finally hit bottom. She didn't need to get drunk, not right now. But she did need to find a way to relax and come to terms with the demise of her family. Nothing had prepared her for this. She'd expected an awkward and strange…maybe just uncomfortable reunion with her estranged family. And now she had a putrid excuse for a man demanding she leave with him.

The man remained next to her, his huge shoulders imposing in presence, leaning toward Vallah. "What's your name, woman?"

She held her breath in defense of his foul stench. If she attempted to ignore him, he could get irritated. An irritated man wasn't what she needed right now. "Vallah."

"You and your cousin had the same name?" The barmaid now looked at her with suspicion. Her eyes squinted as she wiped down the counter.

"Yeah, it was a family thing. I think our grandmother was named Vallah and we were named after her." *Shit, shit,*

shit! I hadn't thought of an alias.

The large woman shrugged. "Yeah, you can't be the same Vallah, or you'd have your breeder mark...and I don't see a scar, so you can't be her."

The guy with the big shoulders laughed. "It doesn't matter if you're a breeder or not. I'm claiming you." His dark brown eyes opened wider. "It's been a long time for me, sweetheart. Hope you've got some spunk."

The thought of this vile creature anywhere near her made her want to vomit. Still, she tried to ignore him as she figured a way out of this mess. She'd been in town five minutes and some degenerate had already tried to claim her. She could kill him in an instant, but not there...not with witnesses.

"Your auntie had secrets...I wonder if you have any. We'll see what I can ferret out. Come with me." He grabbed her wrist.

"Over my dead body!" She jerked her wrist out of his hand and returned with a chop to the throat.

He grabbed his neck and began coughing, face reddening as he fought for oxygen.

"Ma'am, we don't want trouble. You should just go with him. It's his right." An older man came out of a back room.

She nearly protested, but thought better of it. This guy would be easier to get rid of outside. "Of course, I'm sorry. It's been a long day; you know?" She reached into her bag and pulled out some money, throwing it on the bar.

"My name's Marcus." He coughed and wheezed. "Get used to calling it out." He growled as he snatched her by the back of the neck. She knew of at least eight ways to break his arm from that position. Waiting to teach this wretch a lesson was the real challenge.

An even bigger man than the disgusting creature holding her stepped in front of them. His suit was spotless, his beard trimmed tight to his face, and baby blue eyes smiled at Vallah. "I'm sorry, sir, but you can't have her." He looked at her again and nodded. "Vallah, what have I told you about going out without me? Until we get your marker, men aren't going to know you're mine."

"I'm sorry. I tried to argue, but he wouldn't listen." Who was this stranger and why was he helping her?

She stared at the man, knowing she didn't recognize him. Sure, he was an attractive man, but he was much larger than the guy who tried to claim Vallah first. At least the guy holding her would be an easy kill. The larger guy could do some damage, yet she didn't feel any fear. If anything, she wanted to see him without the suit. Maybe being claimed by him wouldn't be so bad. At least he had decent hygiene.

No. She had a task...an assignment from her masters. She was "chosen." Still, she'd rather take on the bigger guy. He, at least, didn't make her want to vomit.

"I claimed her, she's mine!" Marcus growled.

The larger man stepped closer. "Release my woman now and we don't have to settle this in a less than civilized manner." He held up his hands and took a step back. "Where are my manners? You said your name was Marcus?"

"What of it?" he asked as he tightened the grip on her neck.

"My name is William. William Pendleton."

Marcus immediately dropped his hand from her neck. "M-M-Mister Pendleton, sir. I'm sorry, of course she's yours."

Okay, so he's some sort of big shot around here.

"It's an honest mistake. Here," he said, pulling out a money clip, "you're obviously a little tense. Go down to the house on the corner, ask for Jennifer. She does magical things...things that will curl your toes." He winked at the man and looped his arm in hers. "Come, dear, let's get you home."

Poor Jennifer.

CHAPTER THREE

"Your first day back home and you almost get yourself claimed by the town lunatic." William shook his head. "Nice work, Vallah."

"I'm sorry, do we know each other?" She kept her face as blank as possible as she willingly climbed into his craft. He closed the door behind her, walked around the front and climbed in. He punched coordinates into the dashboard and didn't speak until they were off the ground and moving.

"I was a friend of your mother's. We had a deal. When her indicator alerted me to your arrival—"

"Your what?"

"Indicator. A sensor that tells me when the transport device is activated. Anyway, when it alerted me to your arrival, I went to town to wait. I figured if I saw my home destroyed, I'd need a stiff drink. Anyway, you found trouble before I could get to the only watering hole within walking distance of your family's property."

She looked out the window as she concentrated on what to do next. "Where are we going?"

"Home, of course. Where else is there?" He pressed a button on the dash, which must have been some sort of communication device. "Wanda, I'm bringing a wife home. Please ready my room."

"Wife?" Her heart erupted into a rhythm she couldn't count. *Shit! I've been claimed!*

"Relax. It's just for show. I have no intentions of forcing you into anything. But if you're claimed by me, no other man will claim you." That wouldn't be so bad. He at least smelled nice and looked fine in a suit.

"What are you, exactly? What kind of pull do you have?"

He laughed and undid the top button of his shirt. "I own most of this town, including the sex workers. I keep a detailed list of newly registered breeders to ensure that the elite get a mate of their choosing. I also run the underground."

That was a lot to take in. What exactly was the underground? And this guy...this guy would have paired off her sister.

"How many wives do you have?" She gulped. Did he expect her to become part of his harem?

"Just you."

"Are you gay?"

His laughter burst and echoed within the small chamber. "Jesus Christ! No, I'm not gay. But I'm not into forcing women to fuck, got it? So just relax. Your mother trusted me. You should too. We knew I'd have this position one day. She saved my life once. All she asked for in return was that I protect you. I was her Plan B."

Vallah had only been eleven when she'd left, and too young to understand the workings of politics. She didn't know who this man was, or whether her mother actually trusted him, or if he had intel from her torture. Why didn't she mention him on her recording? *Wait, she did say she'd have someone waiting...*

The remainder of the ride was silent, until the locking mechanism clutched his transport vehicle. His smell invaded the vehicle when he undid the top button to his shirt. He smelled deliciously warm and spicy. She stole glances of him when she could. He wasn't just tall, he was lean, the jacket tight around his arms and shoulders. His thighs looked strong through the pants as well.

"Look, since the servants think we just got married, there will be…expectations. Just play along. You'll have to sleep in my room tonight, but you have my word, I won't force myself on you. Understood? But when you climb out of this hovercraft, you need to be the excited bride that just landed the hottest bachelor in the region. You're already a little old to be claimed, so it will be a tough sell. Think you can handle that?"

There were no thespians among the Amazons. She'd had no acting lessons. But subterfuge was a lesson that was taught well. "Yes, I can manage. Just one thing first." Reaching up, she placed her hands on the sides of his face. Choking down her fear, she leaned in and planted her lips on his. She could feel the shock as his muscles tensed, then relaxed. His tongue graced her lips and she parted them, accepting him in. He smelled wonderful, clean, and he tasted like mint.

When she released him, his face was red. "Wow, I, uh…"

"Thank you for saving me. I didn't want your people recognizing a first kiss, so I thought it best to thank you while getting that out of the way. I mean, we're paired now, right?" If the wetness in her panties was any indicator…it might not be a bad thing. Even if he was the bad guy, she hadn't had any pleasure in over a year. It couldn't hurt to at least sample him.

The doors opened and ten servants lined up, hands folded behind them. "Mr. Pendleton, your bride's quarters are prepared. The cake will be delivered, and dinner will be ready in twenty minutes."

"Very well. You are dismissed."

She took his hand for appearance's sake and followed him to her new room. It made her long for her hut with the Amazons. Everything was white and sterile. Marble floors were accented with glass tables. A person could sustain a long list of injuries with the hard surfaces in this room.

"The shower is over there. You'll find something, uh, more suitable to wear in the closet over there." His arm extended, and she followed his line of sight to a massive closet full of women's clothes. Why did he have women's clothes if she was his only 'wife'?

"What if they don't fit?"

"They'll shrink to your size. That's how they were designed. Right now, you look like a warrior from an obscure television show. Shower and change before meeting me in the dining area." He gave a curt nod before turning on his heel.

"William?"

By the time he turned, she was less than a foot away, startling him when he managed to turn around. "Uh"—he took a step back— "yes?"

"I am a warrior woman. I've been trained to kill. That's where I've been for the past decade…learning how to kill in the most efficient manner." She cocked her brow. "And I like my clothes. Okay?"

His lips tightened into a thin line in what looked like a stifled grin. "You'll wear something appropriate to dinner. After that, wear what you want. There are nightclothes in the closet for sleeping."

"I don't wear clothes to bed." She closed the ten inches between them, commanding control. He had to understand who was in charge.

"Dinner is waiting on you to get cleaned up." Without another word, or anymore posturing, he closed the door behind him.

A shower didn't sound like a rotten idea, so she walked into the bathroom and disrobed. The water startled her when it sprayed automatically. Dispensers shot soap at her in a predetermined amount, and the shower was finished with a floral scent she didn't like. *You can't sneak up on someone when you smell like a flower garden. Idiots.*

Once dried, she headed to the closet to choose something to wear to dinner. This wasn't what she'd expected…what she'd trained for. She was going to eat, then get back to her room to make a plan. She had to find her sister and get her out of whatever hell she was in. But she barely remembered the town. How was she going to find the mayor's mansion?

Frustrated, she snatched a black dress from a hanger and pulled it on. As expected, it hung off her like a wet sack. A silver pin caught her attention, and when she brushed her finger over it, the dress instantly shrank to her size. Clothing had come a long way since her departure.

She stepped up to a mirror and was trying to decide what to do with her sopping wet hair when gadgets shot out of the counter at her. A dryer blew her hair out in seconds, a mask sprayed her face with makeup, and another wand came down, securing her hair in a twist. Her reflection looked like something out of an old political ad.

She wanted to vomit. "From warrior to politician's wife. Great." With a deep sigh, she slid on shoes she found in the closet, which also formed to her feet, before heading to dinner. How many women would have loved this shit? She wanted her leather pants, her vest, and her weapons. Not some stupid black frilly dress and a French twist.

Her shoes clacked against the marble floor as she found her way to the dining room. William sat patiently waiting at the head of a very large table. He couldn't hide the shock on his face. Apparently politician's wife was his type.

"Have a seat."

Fighting the urge to tell him she'd sit when she felt like it, she reluctantly pulled the chair out and parked her ass. The food on the table did smell delicious.

"There are two glasses of wine because I didn't know if you preferred red or white."

She lifted the silver dome off the plate and stared down at the sight before her. Three shrimp lay on a bed of leaves.

"What's this?" It couldn't possibly be considered a meal. A snack, maybe. But she needed ample amounts of protein to keep her strength.

"It's called the first course." He sighed before stabbing into a shrimp and taking a bite.

"You're joking. How many courses are there?"

"Six. Why?" She could feel the frustration oozing from his every cell.

"I'm a very curious person, William." She looked at him from across the long table. "And I don't want to miss the main course." The glass of red wine looked inviting, so she grabbed it, tossed her silverware on her plate, and carried it down to the seat closest to him. "There, now I don't have to shout."

He laughed. "You are a peculiar creature."

Popping a shrimp in her mouth, she shrugged. "What's so peculiar about me?"

He held on to his wine glass and gazed at the table momentarily. "Women who have just been claimed usually keep their distance. The first mating is usually…unpleasant. Yet here you are, sitting close, challenging me. Don't get me wrong, most expect my claim to be pleased, but still."

Chewing on her third and final shrimp, she looked around the room. "There are twenty-eight things in here I could use as a weapon, ten of which could dish a deadly blow on the first strike. Sure, you're larger than me, but that makes you slower. I could probably hit you four or five times before you swung on me. Judging by those hands, you're not much of a fighter. All of the callouses are on your palms, which means you use a weight machine to stay in shape. You are not someone I fear, sir."

He stared at her, speechless.

Two servants brought in the next course, clearing out

the first plates. Soup. It was too salty and was mostly just broth. She didn't enjoy it in the least.

William placed his spoon next to his bowl and folded his hands under his chin. "Vallah, what are your plans?"

The truth wasn't all that dangerous. "I haven't formed them yet. The status of my parents and our home has thrown a wrench into the plans I had, but finding my sister is the first step."

"Very well, we'll go there first thing in the morning."

Was this guy for real? She wasn't going to have to do recon, hunt around his house for maps…he was just going to take her there? "You know the mayor?"

Servants interrupted again, bringing salad and bread. As soon as they were out of earshot, William answered.

"I helped put him in that position, so yes, I know the mayor. Our arrival will be of no surprise. But…when your sister recognizes you, she'll out you. You know that, yes? She turned on your parents. What makes you think she won't do the same to you?"

"But that won't matter since you claimed me already…right?"

"Wrong. You had a tattoo. You no longer do. They're going to want to know why. They will want to know where you've been."

"They who?" Who was in charge? What would they do with that information?

"I could have the tattoo replaced. That would reduce suspicion. Can you come up with a cover story for your disappearance?"

She squinted at him. Why was he helping her? What did her mother do, or not do, to gain his loyalty?

"Vallah, you need a cover story, and you'd better make it good."

"Agreed. I'll think about it tonight." She was not going to bear the mark of a breeder, of that much she was certain. But the rest…the rest needed ironing out. "Again, I ask who 'they' is…are. Who are they?"

"Much has changed in the last decade. The government has grown to a point where they outnumber us. Every single aspect of our lives is regulated...except the claiming or marriage. The man claims the woman and that's that. You've been missing for a decade. Your parents were questioned and tortured. Breeders are coming up missing at an alarming rate and the elite are irate. They want to know why, where they are going, and who is taking them. They will think you have the answers, putting whoever did help you at risk."

"They'll never find them."

Shock painted every inch of his face. "So you do know something?"

She nodded. "And I'll die keeping it a secret."

"Vallah, they have...ways. I can't keep you safe if you can't come up with a verifiable story, or at a minimum, a believable one."

Something in her snapped. She wanted William naked. She wanted him inside of her. It was like she was an animal in heat. The temperature around her neck increased, her breasts felt heavy. Warmth and moisture pooled between her legs, begging for a void to be filled. He wanted to talk about plans...she just wanted him. She wanted to dominate him...hear him beg.

What is wrong with me?

She tried to focus. "Are there still mountains in Tennessee?"

His lips spread into a smile. "Why yes, those are still mostly untouched."

She nodded and smiled. "My mother had a sister, and she whisked me away to Tennessee to hide up in the mountains so I wouldn't be claimed at such a tender age. She thought it best that I be able to grow up before having to deal with breeding. Now that I'm all grown up, I came home to be with the mate she chose for me... a suitable one. Can you play along with that story without it backfiring?"

"Yes, and I was very angry that my promised mate disappeared. I can even claim to have ordered your parents' incarceration. They violated my rights." He cleared his throat. "Just so we're clear, that's a total lie. I was shocked and very worried for your mother when I found out she was taken."

"Good. Now I don't have to kill you."

William looked as if he might fall off his chair.

A servant wheeled in a cart with larger trays. This time, a beautiful roasted turkey was revealed. She served Vallah first, only two small slices, then four for William. After a dollop of mashed potatoes and three solitary green beans were placed on her plate, the woman left.

"Oh, if we're going to be together for any amount of time, these people need to feed me."

William laughed as she cut a large chunk off the turkey and plopped it on her plate.

He shook his head. "You know, it's odd that my new wife has been the only person to threaten my life no less than three times in one evening. You're setting a record here."

She ignored his ribbing. "Do all women eat like birds here?"

"Do all women eat like linebackers wherever you were?" He smiled as he sipped at his wine.

She nodded while she chewed. She washed the turkey down with her wine. "Yes, they do. When you develop a good amount of lean muscle, you need a lot of protein to keep it. You don't see any frail women where I was." *Shit. Stop talking!*

His gaze locked on hers for a brief moment before he broke the connection and finished his plate. "The mark, it's going to bother you, isn't it?"

"Why would a mark that says some man can force me to start making babies by the time I'm sixteen bother me?" She didn't mean to roll her eyes at him. But it was too late.

"Fourteen."

She dropped her fork. "Excuse me?"

"Doctors have determined that it's safe for most fourteen-year-old women to give birth."

"Children," she corrected. "Fourteen-year-old *girls* are *still* children!" Her heart started to race. Was her sister married off at fourteen? The thought of some disgusting creature like Marcus hovering over her fourteen-year-old sister made her ill. The appetite was gone. "Marrying them off at fourteen is bad enough, but impregnating them?"

She had to find Faith. She had to be okay.

"Tell me about this mayor. Does he treat her well?" *Please say yes. Please.*

The sound of another cart entering the room made her want to scream. She needed answers.

"Sir, your wedding cake." The woman brushed her hands down her uniform. "Congratulations on your union."

"We'll take it from here. Just pour the coffee and clear the dinner plates." He folded his hands in his lap as he waited for his servant to finish.

Vallah searched his face for some indication as to the answer to her question. When the servant woman finally closed the dining room door, he leaned in. "She was married off at seventeen. At first, she seemed very unhappy. Then, out of the blue, she started coming out in public, wearing expensive clothing. She smiles a lot. And, if I must say, she seems to enjoy the role of mayor's wife quite well. I don't think he mistreats her."

Collapsing against the back of the chair, the air she had been holding escaped her lungs. She was okay. At least, there didn't seem to be any immediate dangers. Her betrayal would have to be sorted out, but there was time for that.

"While I'm certain you're not in the mood for wedding cake, we must..."

Pushing away from the table, she smiled before she stood. "Allow me." A million thoughts ran through her head as she looked at the small wedding cake. It was pretty elaborate, with fake diamonds dotting the fake stitching. It looked like a fluffy, edible, jewel-encrusted pillow. Inside, the cake was red, deep red, like blood. A chocolate ganache filling separated two delicate layers. She handed him his slice of bloody wedding cake.

"Thank you. My, uh, artist will be here soon. We have to make your mark look aged. He's a master at this sort of thing. It will be pain free. The wedding mark is fairly standard. It goes on your left hand, same as old-time wedding rings did, except the ring finger is encircled and it goes up the back of your hand and around your wrist. It's 3-D, a new art form. Because of who I am, it must be done this way, though my understanding is that there is some burning at first." His lips curved down into a frown. "Truly, I am sorry we have to do it this way."

"Because it burns?" She couldn't imagine what other reason he'd have to be sorry.

He stood from his seat and walked behind it, gripping it. "Because it will hurt you, yes. Because I'm sure that whatever you had to do to remove the breeder mark was already painful. Mostly because I can only imagine how much distaste you'll have for me for making you put it back on."

Was this guy for real? So far, he'd saved her—not that she'd needed it—from a psychopath. He'd given her shelter, food, a fancy dress she hated, but most of all, it seemed anyway that he'd provided her with safety and cover.

"Sit down. Eat this crazy-looking cake so I can get out of this dress." She smiled and took a large bite of cake. The red must have been whatever they used to make the cake taste like cherry. The cherry cake and chocolate ganache were rich together, but very tasty. She only took a few bites before the sweetness was too much for her.

"Mr. Pendelton, sir. You have a visitor." A small male servant stood stiffly at the entry to the dining area.

"Very well," he said as he waved his hand. "You and the others may go home now."

It was the underground artist that would replace her breeder mark. With a deep breath, she stood, grabbing the decanter of wine and her glass. "Let's get this over with."

With one curt nod, he stood and led her out of the dining area, through a complicated maze of halls until they reached a wooden door. When he pushed it open, she found one reclining chair with two lights shining on it. A man sat in a wheeled stool readying his tools. "Nice to meet you, Mrs. Pendleton. Please, have a seat."

"I'll hold these for you," William said as he took the decanter and glass from her hands.

After taking a seat in the reclining chair, she held up her hand and William handed over the glass of wine. She wished for something a bit stronger.

The little man on the stool looked at her left arm where her mark should have been. "I don't understand. I thought you said she'd had the mark removed? There's no scarring."

"The person who did it was very skilled and had advanced technology." Well, it was sort of the truth.

He cocked his bushy eyebrow at her. He was older, hair nearly white with darkness still peppered in. "You say you were marked ten years ago?"

"Yes."

He rifled through a large black case, looking at little plastic bottles before finally pulling one out that satisfied him. "This was the ink used a decade ago. Now, it won't hurt at all. Just sit back and relax. You might feel some buzzing." He squirted the contents of the plastic bottle into a large black patch, and then smoothed it over her arm.

She felt a slight buzzing sensation where the patch stuck on, just like he had warned. It wasn't painful, just a feeling of vibration.

Next, he took a small box and slid her left hand inside,

up to her wrist. "There's a small handle in there. Grip that, please."

Feeling the small handle, she circled her fingers around it.

"This burns a bit, but I've yet to draw a tear." He patted her knee. "You ready?"

After emptying the contents of her glass, she gave him a nod. Her stomach tightened as she waited for the searing pain to start. The only sensation was warmth that tickled up and down the path of her marital mark.

"It's not so bad, really." With no real pain to speak of, her muscles relaxed. The warmth increased to hot, but no hotter than the water she used to clean dishes.

The man removed the patch on her arm. The disgusting breeder mark was there, slightly faded, of course. When he removed the device on her hand, she was actually astonished. A three-dimensional image stood out on her ring finger with a huge gem on top. The gold trailed up her hand until it connected with a gem-encrusted bracelet. It was part of her...embedded in her skin. This was it...she'd been marked..

CHAPTER FOUR

William paid the man in something called credits and he immediately left. Vallah stayed in the chair for a brief moment, trying to accept what she'd just allowed to happen. If it was just for show, why did it give her such a burning sensation in the pit of her stomach?

"Why don't you go rest now? I'll sleep on the sofa or something." A warm hand rested on her shoulder.

She closed her eyes, holding them closed until the count of three, then opened them as she stood. "I'm not all that tired. I just want to get this dress off. Show me how to get back." As if she hadn't already memorized the way. A few more rooms and she'd have the entire blueprint in her head already.

With a gentle smile, he turned and walked out of the room with her on his heel. Her eyes darted around from doorway to doorway as they made their way to their room. His scent trailed behind him; the heady spice made her heart flutter, which did nothing more than irritate her. She'd never been this distracted by a man.

They passed a study, a room with exercise equipment, a sitting room, and then the dining area they'd just left, which was already cleared out, and then back down the original hall, which housed several bedrooms. When they finally reached the room they were to share, he sat on the edge of the bed and gazed at the floor.

"We need to discuss something."

No, I need time to think, to devise a plan to free my sister and figure out where to go. Maybe I can find my way back to the transporter and to the Amazon women who trained me. I am lost and in terrible need of direction.

"Please." His voice was low, in a near whisper.

She sat on the floor and looked up at him. "Go on."

"I killed a man once, quite by accident. Your mother…she saw the whole thing. Had I been discovered, it would have meant the death penalty. She helped me hide the body and cover up my crime. She saved me." He closed his eyes tight. Maybe the memories were too much. "The point is; I owe my life—my very freedom—to your mother. She said something big was in store for me. How she knew that, I had no idea. But she knew. You had just been born. Man, she was so young."

"William? The point?"

He took a deep breath and let it out, his shoulders falling slightly. "The point would be that she only made me promise two things. The first was to keep you safe up on your return if something should happen to her. The second was that I keep my hands off of you."

Her mother was guarding her celibacy? "That makes no sense. You said I was just a baby. How could she have known?"

"Because, your father wasn't your biological father. You were implanted."

Her chest ached like she had just received a blow to the sternum. "I'm sorry. What? That can't be right. I look just like her, and one has nothing to do with the other." And how did any of that answer her question? Was it his guilt that made him speak about her father?

He smiled. "Yes. Yes, you do. You are hers, biologically. And before you get angry, she never strayed from her husband. But medically, her egg was blended with the DNA of someone not your father. Someone who hadn't been tainted by the vaccine. That's all I know. They put the embryo in her and you appeared nine months later. She knew you'd be fertile. That was the plan."

"Wait. Wait just a minute. You knew her before I was born, and you were old enough to have murdered someone. How old are you…exactly?" She moved to her feet, nervous energy making her twitchy.

"Fifty-two. The vaccine slowed the rate of aging. That's why I look almost half my age." He rubbed his forehead with the pads of his fingers. "It's been a very long fifty-two years."

When he finally had the courage to look at her, she shrugged. "You're still attractive. Age isn't really what it used to be. I mean, look at the breeders, becoming mothers at such a tender age. Being forced to consummate a marriage they had no say in. I'm thankful the people who, uh, cared for me wouldn't allow me to even experiment until I was eighteen. Even then, I probably wasn't mature enough." She sat next to him, placing her hand on his forearm. "What's with the speech and guilt? You're worried about our marriage? Seems silly since we just met and our marriage is fake. Is it the sex? You want to have sex?"

"What? No. I wouldn't even if you asked me to. Our dinner was laced with pheromones." He sprung up from the bed and paced. "That's the problem. I've been single all of this time because…because the old ways are gone. We force women to marry us, force them into sex, either by physical force or lacing their food so they feel like it's their idea. And I don't blame my staff; it's a cultural norm now. It's disgusting. My parents were in love. They wanted to be together."

She'd been drugged. *Great. No wonder I kept panting like a cat in heat.* Every time she smelled William, she had thoughts of stripping him naked.

"And you want that too?" This man was puzzling her. He seemed more emotional than anyone she'd met.

"Of course I do, but dating doesn't happen. Not unless you're part of the underground." His shoulders slumped forward more, making him look deflated.

Comfort wasn't something she'd been given or been taught in the last decade. Vallah had no idea what to do for him or why he looked so defeated. "Wait…you said you were in charge or in control of the underground." That was it…he was in love with someone there. And now…he was married to *her*.

He only nodded, confirming her suspicion.

"You're right. Let's get some rest. You look exhausted. Tomorrow, we'll go see my sister." She brushed the pin on the dress to loosen it and headed to the closet to find something to wear to bed. While she wasn't used to sleeping with clothes on, she didn't want to make the guy any more uncomfortable than she already had.

She found a suitable track suit and slid it on, kicking the heels into the closet and closing the door. William was still fully clothed and lying on the bed with his back facing her. A loud thud came from the hall. He leapt from the bed. She ran, grabbing her fighting sticks out of her pile of personal belongings.

"What are those?"

"Never mind, open the door," she whispered.

"No!" His tone was harsh, but low. "Someone is out there."

She rolled her eyes. "Exactly, and they're not going to leave. So open the door." She nodded toward the door, giving him a look that she hoped said that he should open the door before she hit him with one of her sticks.

Slowly, he turned the handle, then pulled the door toward him. It exploded open, knocking him on his ass. A man stood with a black bag in his left hand and a wand of some sort in his right. Whatever the wand was, it shone bright blue.

Vallah squared off with the intruder. She stepped to the right, and he stepped closer in her direction. *Good, I can gauge his stride.* He took a swipe at her with the large wand. She leapt back, and while his weight followed the motion of his arm, she spun around, striking a blow between his shoulder blades. When he arched his back, she took another swipe behind his legs, dropping him to his knees.

"Vallah!" William shouted.

White-hot pain burned through her back, stunning her briefly. She threw her weight forward, separating her from whatever was burning. Another man stood with a wand in his hand. "Trying to stun me? Try again!" She kicked her foot straight out in front, landing a blow to the man's chest. The man on his knees immediately behind her, she kicked backward, sending his face to the ground and his wand skidding across the floor. Quickly, she knocked him on his temple and he blacked out.

Her other assailant was more determined and rushed at her. She sidestepped, wrapping his arm under hers, then twisted, dislocating his elbow. The wand dropped to the floor. "Quick, I need rope or something to tie them up."

William's eyes were wide as he stared at her.

"I said quickly. Now! Get something!" Snatching up one of the wands, she touched it to the man's head. He fell immediately to the floor.

"Shit, you killed him!" William mouth fell open as he stared at the man she'd just stunned.

"I did?"

He nodded. "You can't touch it to someone's head. The shock is too much."

She walked over to the one unconscious man lying on the floor and touched the wand to his temple.

"What are you doing?" William screamed as he scrambled to his feet.

"What do you think they were here to do, bake us cookies?" She ran to her things and grabbed her short sword. "Lock the door and don't open it until I return.

Jesus, don't you have security?"

He stared at the bodies on the floor.

"William!" When his head snapped toward her, she spoke calm and slow. "Lock the door."

He nodded.

Vallah crept down the hall, visually scanning each room as she passed, hearing footsteps ahead. Luckily, her bare feet made no noise on the marble floor as she moved quickly toward the next assailant.

"She's here. Tom and Ron are in the bedroom now," the man whispered into his wrist. It must have been some sort of communicator. "Roger that. We'll get her bagged and to you immediately, Mr. Mayor."

Damn.

The man's back was to her. She could have easily thrown her sword and impale him, but dead men didn't give answers. Looking around, she found a large grandfather clock five feet on the other side of the door. She crept behind it and threw her stick on the other side. The man came out; no wand was in his hand. Fast as she could, she leaped on his back, threw her left arm around his neck, and pulled hard on her wrist with her right hand. Locking her legs around his waist, she squeezed. He fell backward, both of them crashing to the floor. The marble crushed against her back as she held on tight to the man who was struggling to get oxygen to his body.

The gurgling sound told her he'd black out soon enough. Holding on for a few more seconds, she felt his body go limp and released him immediately. After pushing him off of her, she loosened the tie around his neck and pulled it free, then used it to bind his hands behind his back.

She dragged him down the hall to William's room and knocked on the door. "Open up, it's me."

The door swung open, and William's face was devoid of any color. "You killed another one?"

"Nope, this one still breathing. He's just unconscious.

Find something to bind his feet." She pulled the heavy man inside the door and locked it behind her. William handed her a pair of stockings.

"For a man without a wife, you sure have a lot of women's clothes." Shaking her head, she tied the man's feet together. "Help me get him into the shower."

Once in the shower, she ordered William to turn the water on cold.

The man woke up coughing. "B-b-b-bitch."

The insult made her smile. "Indeed. Why did you come to bag me?"

He stared into her eyes and smiled. "Fuck you."

The cold water poured on him, spraying her arm in the meantime. It wouldn't take but a minute more and his whole body would start to shiver. She began unbuttoning his shirt.

"W-w-what are you d-d-doing?" His bottom jaw started to shake.

Good, he's cold.

She didn't answer until she had his entire abdomen exposed. "You can turn the water off, William." Once the water was off, she turned back to the man. "I one read about how the ancient Chinese used a form of death sentence called Death by a Thousand Cuts. You're about to experience what that feels like."

"Vallah!" William gasped. "You've killed the other two. Enough already."

"Shush!" she barked at him. "How many of you are there?"

"F-f-fu-fuck you, b-b-bitch!"

Dragging her blade across him, she began to push, and sliced a two-inch cut into his left pectoral. Blood trickled down his chest in watery lines. "One."

He cried out in pain.

"Oh, you're a sissy. That's only the first one." She made another slice on his other pectoral.

Sounds of retching came from behind her. William lost

his dinner.

"Three," she said as she sliced into his nipple.

"Okay, okay, there were three of us. That's all." He began to cry.

She sliced him again.

"Oh, God! I answered! I answered!"

Wiping his blood off her knife onto his pants, she smiled at him. "Why does the mayor want me bagged?"

"The mayor?" William repeated.

"How did you know?" The man stopped shivering.

"William, water."

She could see him hesitate before he pushed the button for cold water.

"Okay! Okay!" the man yelled again. "He wants to find out where you've been!"

With a cocked brow, she shook her head. "He could've just called. Why kidnap me from my new husband's bed?"

"I d-d-don't know. I'm just following orders!" the man cried.

This cut went to his bicep. His cries of agony were getting to William.

"Vallah, please stop." His hand was on her shoulder.

"Not until I have my answers." She looked up at William, whose color had turned slightly gray. "You don't have to stay for this."

"What do you want to know?" the man asked. "I don't want to die!"

She stood up and turned the water off. "Everything you know. Now."

"Mr. Mayor heard you were spotted in a bar and that William came to retrieve you. Since you haven't been seen in so long, he wanted to know for himself. I don't know why he wanted you taken. That's all I know."

"And my sister?"

"She's the one that told us to use the bag." He cried. "Please, no more. Please."

After leading William out of the bathroom, she closed

the door behind her. "Is there somewhere we can hide?"

The color started returning to his face. "The underground."

"I'm going to change. I suggest you do too. There's blood on your shirt." She started pulling off the track suit as he pulled off his shirt.

Once dressed in her leather pants, boots, and vest, she pulled on her wrist covers.

"What are those?" he asked.

"To protect me from blades. The leather is special. It can't be cut once it's cured. A simple swipe of a sword or knife will be absorbed by the material, protecting my arm. I don't know what we're headed into, but I'm not taking any chances."

She slung the strap to her bag over her neck, with the bag resting on her hip. On the way down the hall, she scooped up her fighting stick and crammed it in the holder on her other side.

William guided her to a set of stairs leading down.

"Where are we going? Isn't your transportation on the roof?"

"The one below doesn't have a tracking chip in it. It's how I move around undetected. As far as the police can tell, I'll still be at home."

For someone so sensitive to violence, he seemed okay with subterfuge. Once they reached a garage below the house, he pulled the door open to his craft and held it for her. Once inside, he climbed in the other door.

"This one is much smaller," she noted aloud.

"The idea is to blend in, not stand out." He punched coordinates into the dash before turning to her. "Look, things got way out of hand in there. The stuff you did…that's…you're okay with killing and torturing people?"

He must have thought her a monster. "No, not at all. I'm okay hurting people who mean to do me harm. It evens the scales. Men don't expect women to be able to defend themselves. Violence begets violence and whatnot. I'm sorry you had to see that side of me."

He held out his palms in surrender. "I'm not used to women being that physical, but please don't take it as an insult or judgment. That was just...that was insane in there. Cutting him like that. Why?"

She sat back and crossed her arms over her chest. "Do you think he would have told me the truth if I'd asked nicely?"

"Fair point." He closed his eyes briefly. Once he gathered his thoughts, he opened them again. "Is it strange that I'm aroused?"

"According to old world psychologists, near-death experiences increase sexual desire. So no, you're not strange."

"I don't want or need to know how you learned what old world psychologists knew. Any old reference material was deemed illegal a millennium ago." He turned his head to look through the front glass. "We'll be there in a second. Listen, the people down here are...distrusting of anything they don't know. Don't take their hostility personally. Stay with me and we'll be fine."

Laughter erupted from her before she could contain it. "Sorry, but as you can see, I'll be fine either way."

They entered some sort of concrete tunnel when the vehicle came to a stop. After cutting the power, he jumped out. She followed his lead.

"This way," he whispered.

She followed him down a set of metal stairs and to a door. To her surprise, he didn't go through the door, but crawled under the stairwell and moved a box out of the way, revealing a hidden passage.

"Nice."

Once inside, he pulled the box behind them, concealing the entrance. They both stood up, and Vallah was barely able to absorb what her eyes were seeing. It was an elaborate underground city. She'd expected to see filthy, poor, homeless people. What she found were rows and rows of tiny houses, shops, and even a candy shop. William led her to one particular house, the door painted black. He knocked.

The woman who opened the door was stunning. She stood almost six feet tall, and she matched Vallah in height. Her thick, dark hair held a slight curl that framed a face that was near perfection. Her emerald eyes were offset against flawless alabaster skin. No wonder he was in love with her. She had a scar that ran the length of her left arm...the scar from having the breeder mark removed.

"William!" She threw her arms around him and kissed his cheek before releasing him and looking at Vallah. "Who do we have here?" Her gaze traced the length of her arm and to her 3-D matrimonial mark. "Oh."

"Vallah, this is Karen. Karen, my wife, Vallah." His face burned red.

Vallah held out her hand, surprised when cool skin met her warm palm. "Very nice to meet you, Karen."

Without hesitation, Karen turned Vallah's hand over and looked at the gems embedded in her skin.

"Don't worry, it's just for show. His heart still belongs to you." She hoped her words would ease whatever discomfort she was causing.

"You must be joking," Karen said with a laugh.

"Uh, no?" She looked back and forth between them.

"I'm his sister, nitwit. Come in." She pulled the door open wider.

"Really?" he whispered over his shoulder.

Her shoulders rose and fell in a halfhearted shrug. Vallah knew his heart belonged elsewhere. It was just the wrong woman.

Karen poured three cups of dark coffee, placing them on the kitchen table. "So what brings you down here?"

William rubbed his forehead as he leaned in on his elbows. "Snow tried to black bag her. Three thugs broke into our house."

"Oh my God, William! How did you two escape?" She put her hand on his forearm, and then glanced at Vallah. "Neither one of you have a mark on you."

He looked at Vallah, searching. She didn't see the harm in telling her the truth. Vallah would be gone soon, in hiding with her sister. She gave him an affirmative nod.

"Vallah killed two of them. The other is tied up in my shower. I didn't know where else to go or what to do." He took a deep breath and released it. "My life is ruined."

"Now wait a damned minute," Vallah spat. "There has to still be law enforcement and courts, right? Those men broke into your house and meant to do you harm. It was self-defense."

Karen shook her head. "You're not from around here, are you?"

"That's not the way it works, Vallah. Not anymore." He looked so tired. His eyes were starting to puff out, and his hair was a mess from constantly running his fingers through it.

"William, we can't solve this right this very second. Why don't you go lie down and let me get to know my sister-in-law?" Karen's smile looked forced as she glanced at Vallah, then back to William. "You always think clearly after a nap."

With a heavy sigh, he scooted his chair from the table and left the room.

Karen didn't speak until she heard the click of a door closing. "Vallah, was it?"

"Yes, ma'am." *Please don't be a problem. I don't want to hurt you.*

"Do you care to tell me why Snow wants to black bag you and hurt my brother?" Leaning back in her chair, she sipped at her coffee, her gaze never faltering. Vallah could feel heat rising up around her neck.

Not knowing this woman, Vallah wasn't willing to tell her the whole truth. William had been a decent man thus far, but that was no indication whether or not she could trust her. Training told her to trust only herself, but she'd have to tell Karen something. No matter what, she didn't want harm to come to her or to her brother.

"I plan on asking the man myself. As far as your brother goes, I will protect him. I'll tell the truth, that I killed those men. But then we need a cover story for William. Take him somewhere and tie him up. Let him be found. I'll say I did it. His life shouldn't be ruined because of a promise to my mother."

Her eyes grew wide. "You're Valerie's daughter. You're *that* Vallah?"

She hadn't heard her mother's name spoken in so long, it brought the sting of a tear to her eye. "Yes, ma'am. Valerie is, rather *was*, my mother."

"So you know, then? That she's dead?"

The ache in her chest must have reflected on her face.

Karen's features softened. "I'm very sorry. For what it's worth, she's only presumed dead. No one has seen her since they took her."

Her mind went into a dark place, a place where her mother had been tortured for an unknown amount of time before they finally extinguished her light. She could almost hear her screaming, begging for mercy. The whisper of a cup sliding on the table drew Vallah's attention from whatever hell she'd slipped into.

"Yes, well, they don't keep them forever, now do they?" She stood up from her chair, unwilling to give her grief another moment. "Tell me how to get to Snow's mansion and I'll leave you to care for your brother."

Karen looked up at Vallah and smiled. "Yes, my brother, who chooses to marry a total stranger who is about to abandon him. Tell me, why did you think we were together?"

"His heart belongs to someone down here. I just don't know who. You should see to it that they're together. It's my firm belief that he deserves happiness." Her grip on the chair tightened, a sense of urgency pulsing through her veins. "Please. Tell me how to get to Snow."

Karen stared at her in silence, as if contemplating how to proceed. "Very well, follow me."

They reached a room with a large glass table. With a wave of Karen's hand, it lit up into a three-dimensional topographical map. "You are here. The red lines are the tunnels we have that go throughout this sector." She pointed to the far side of the table. "This is Snow's property here. This tunnel will lead you to about three hundred yards from his mansion, which is right inside the fence. Once you're inside, you cannot return through the same tunnel, in the event you are monitored or followed. You'd be jeopardizing this entire underground."

"Don't worry, I'll find another means of escape." She studied the map. "What about this tunnel over here? Why is it yellow?"

"It collapsed. That...that was the tunnel that led to your home. Your mother blew it up when they came knocking so that they couldn't find us through her."

The thought of her mother using explosives was a difficult pill to swallow. She'd always been so docile. Except for the day she sent Vallah away. She'd been quick, decisive, and never faltered. Was there a side to her mother that she'd never known? A side that had been involved in an illegal underground, covering up murders, and blowing stuff up?

That tunnel was close to Snow's property. Which meant...if she could get her sister to the transporter, she could save her from whatever nightmare she'd been living.

"Thank you."

"I'll lead you through the tunnel and stay with you until the exit. You're a stranger here, and I don't want someone thinking you're a spy." She slid on a pair of boots and began lacing them.

Vallah held up her hands in protest. There was no way she wanted to put William or his sister in any more danger. "That's okay, I can manage on my own."

"I'm not worried about you. I'm worried about my people." She laughed. "I don't know what kind of training it takes to subdue three of Snow's men, but here people aren't quite that skilled."

There was little to say to that, so Vallah simply followed her through the underground city, her eyes taking in as much as she could. It was unbelievable, the engineering that had gone into this little hideaway. An entire city underground that looked like any other normal city, the one exception being the lack of sky above.

"So wherever you've been hiding all of these years, is that where the other breeders disappeared to?" Karen didn't look at her as she asked the question. That didn't sit well.

"No." That was all she'd give. Vallah wasn't going to disclose her Amazons to a stranger, no matter how hard the stranger tried or how sincere they seemed to be.

"So you don't know where they went?" She stared at the ground in front of her as they entered a narrow tunnel laced with what looked like plaster.

"I can only assume their mothers tried to protect them the way mine did. The thought of young girls being forced into sex at such a young age is nauseating. No fourteen-year-old girl needs to have babies, or sex with full-grown men. It's disgusting." Her sister…what sort of horrifying life had she led? Was that the reason she'd betrayed her parents? Was she bitter?

Karen's sniffling drew her attention. "You okay?"

"My first son was born when I was fifteen. They only let me hold him for about an hour."

She'd been forced to breed. Vallah could not imagine the damage that had been done to this woman, and many like her. "I'd assumed since your mark was removed that you'd escaped that life."

Wiping the tears on the back of her hand, she held her head up high. "Ten babies by the time I was twenty-two. Ten by three different men. I was either pregnant, nursing, or going through post-partem depression. It was the worst existence ever. You'll forgive me, I wasn't trying to get you to disclose whatever safety these girls have. I just…I wanted to imagine a life where you don't live like that."

"You still spend your time fearing and hating men…hating the Centurions for their false sense of hope and for the chaos they've caused. It's just that where I was…there were hardly any men to fear. It was mostly women in hiding." *True, but doesn't disclose much.*

The air in the tunnel was quite cool, and the light began to dim to where Vallah couldn't see her face very well. It was an uneasy feeling. She'd have to rely on her other senses, because at this point her nerves were on edge.

Vallah wanted to remind this woman that she no longer answered to a man, that's she'd survived. "How'd you escape?"

"William helped me fake my death and brought me down here. He spent those eight years building up the underground so he'd have somewhere safe to hide me. I think watching me go through it is why he's never married. Why he never claimed a woman…because he saw what it did to me."

They finally reached the end of the tunnel. Fighting the urge to hug this woman and offer her some comfort, Vallah placed her palm on her shoulder. "You're a tough woman. Trust me, I've been surrounded by some of the hardest women you'll ever meet, and I see that quality in you. You're a survivor. Please tell your brother how much his help has meant to me. I'll be forever in his debt."

She straightened, standing a bit taller, then pushed the door open. "What the…?"

It should have been dawn, with sun peeking through the trees. But the sky was red as blood. "An astrological event? An eclipse, maybe?" Vallah offered.

But then, she felt odd—lighter, almost light as a feather.

"Go. I'll go check our scanners to see what's going

on." She pushed Vallah through the door. "Godspeed," she whispered as she closed it behind her.

CHAPTER FIVE

She could see the mansion, and made her way quietly through the woods. There were no guards standing around that she could see, but she'd have to be cautious. Snow would be on high alert after his men didn't make it back.

But it was early, and chances were that everyone was still asleep inside the mansion.

Pausing at the edge of the forest, she closed her eyes for a moment of meditation. Her training would serve her well in rescuing her sister *if* she managed to keep her emotions in check. She had not seen Faith since she was eleven.

Will she remember me?

After retrieving her short sword from its holster, she ran across the yard until her back was against the stone façade. *One, two, three*, she counted, slowing her heart rate back to near resting. As she visually scanned the surroundings, she reached her right hand to the door next to her. The knob turned. She guessed with guards and a fence surrounding the property, locks weren't a necessity.

Once inside, she listened for any sounds of stirring. No footsteps, no sounds of any kind were to be heard. She was so far undetected. The house was enormous, and it would take some time to find the room which held Faith. Her heartbeat pounded in her ears with every step she took. Peeking in room by room, she found servants, children, and a man who she suspected was Snow. He lay in an ornate bed, surrounded by pillows and three naked women sleeping in a circle around him. Not one of them was blonde. She barely remembered Faith, but did remember that curly blonde hair.

Killing Snow would have to wait.

She continued to creep further down the hall of bedrooms until she found Faith, sitting on the end of her bed in a robe. Her hair was still long, still blonde, and very curly. Pulling the door slowly closed behind her, Vallah saw her sister's shoulders tense when it clicked shut.

She didn't turn, though. She didn't turn to see who was entering her room. She just sat stiff.

"Faith?"

She stood and turned; the look of horror on her face when she saw Vallah made her heart sink. "Who are you and what are you doing in here?"

"I've come to save you, to get you out of this place," she whispered as she took a few steps closer.

"Stay back!" Faith's hand shook. Obviously, she was full of adrenaline after being startled.

"Faith, you were young when I left, but you have to know who I am. I couldn't forget your blonde hair or those beautiful blue eyes."

Water began filling at the base of her eye. She recognized Vallah.

"Do you remember the willow tree where we played? It's still there." Vallah inched a bit closer.

"Vallah?" she said with a sniff. "Is it really you?"

She nodded. "Do you have some clothes you can put on—quickly?"

"I don't understand. How did you get in here?" She took a step back.

"I'm sure this is unnerving. But I was sent to save you.

This whole time I've been gone, I've been learning how to save you...to get you out of here, away from this life."

The tears dangled from her bottom lid, threatening to spill down her face. "What makes you think I want to leave?"

What? She hadn't planned on this. *Who would want to stay?* "Please, Faith, just come with me. We can sort everything out once I get you out of here."

"You..." Her face fell cold, stiff, the emotion gone. "You abandoned me. Mom chooses you, and you, what? Think I want to run away now? When I live in a mansion and can have anything I want?"

"What? I didn't abandon you. I didn't have a choice. Please, Faith, these things, this stuff around you...at what cost does—?"

Faith reached over and slapped a panel on the wall, which illuminated red under her palm. "You'd better run."

Her sister had sounded an alarm. While Vallah couldn't hear it, she knew what Faith meant. Vallah wasn't going to leave her behind, but the chances of escape with Faith fighting her were slim. With little choice, she charged her sister. Faith slapped at her, connecting a few times before Vallah managed to pinch a nerve in her neck. Faith fell unconscious.

Vallah managed to catch her before she hit the floor. Crouching down, she put the weight of Faith's torso on her back and held on to her behind her knees. She carried her to the door, but upon opening it could hear voices. Coming back the way she entered was out of the question. There was a balcony, though...After sliding the door open to the balcony, she placed her sister in a chair, pulled a small rope from her bag and quickly tied it under Faith's arms, lowering her to the ground before leaping off the balcony herself. The commotion was inside, not outside.

With great haste, she slid the rope off of Faith and put her back on her shoulders. Her sister didn't seem to weigh much, so Vallah ran as fast as she could for the woods.

Glancing at the sky, she became nervous. The darkness had deepened, and the sky looked more like darkened blood by the minute. Was this an omen?

The sound of dogs barking in the distance told her that she didn't have much time. A silent prayer to Mercury to carry her faster gave her a boost in speed. He must have heard her pleas, because Faith had become light as a feather and the sound of her feet pounding against the earth had quieted. They were still moving forward, but Vallah didn't feel she was exerting any effort.

Beams of white light hit the ground in front of her, stopping her dead in her tracks. She darted to the left to escape them. "What kind of technology does Snow have?" she gasped.

She fought for air as she moved forward. *Another five hundred yards and I'll be approaching our property and the safety of the willow.*

Another beam of light hit just next to her. Anxiety filled her to her core. Her chest tightened as her heart slammed against her ribcage. "Dammit!" She cursed and kept running. *Is he trying to kill us?*

Her surroundings were now blinding white, and she was unable to move. This was it. Snow's weapon, whatever it was, had frozen her like a statue. Her vision began to blur. She couldn't feel Faith on her shoulders anymore at all. Vallah couldn't feel Faith's warmth, her arms dangling, swatting her sides with each stride. She felt...nothing.

I'm a dead woman. It had been hard enough to feel emotions after the Amazons had finished her training. Certain she was dead inside, her only glimmer of hope was the devastation she'd felt upon seeing her family home as a pile of rubble. But now, whatever that beam of light held for her was surely her end...her ultimate demise.

She was a marked breeder, and thanks to William's brilliant plan, it would be easy to see as the mark on her arm was a shining billboard to those wanting children. She had a fertile womb at their disposal.

Sure, she was a warrior, but how many men could she fight at once? How long could she hold them all off?

Many of them would die finding out.

CHAPTER SIX

High-pitched screams were the first thing Vallah heard when the light dimmed.

"Someone, sedate that woman!" a male voice bellowed.

She blinked, trying to clear her vision when she started to get the feeling back in her skin, and realized she was completely naked. Naked and vulnerable. She still had fists, elbows, knees, and feet. They'd receive blows from them all before they'd take her.

"No one touch her!" Vallah projected her voice as loud as she could without screaming.

"Whoa, lass. Put down your fists. No one is here to harm you."

Her head snapped in the direction of the voice. She blinked again, her vision began to return.

"You'll be a bit off kilter as you re-molecularize. It's a bit hard on the body the first few times."

"What?" She kept her fists tightened as well as her fighting stance. When she saw a dark figure approach, instinct took over and she swung.

"This has to be her, sir."

The screams continued. Looking over to her left, Vallah saw Faith was on the floor screaming at the top of her lungs. "Where am I? Who are you? What happened to Vallah?"

"I'm right here. Calm down." It was next to impossible to think on her feet with her sister wailing.

"You're not her! You lying bitch!"

Two large men restrained her while a woman smeared a substance on her arm. Faith fell silent, only slight mumbles escaping her lips.

The woman motioned to the men with her fingers. One of them handed her a robe, which she began slipping over Faith's shoulders. "Let's get her dressed and to the medical bay. This one is going to take some adjustment."

"Don't take her anywhere!" Vallah demanded. "Leave her there."

Looking around, it was clear she was no longer in the woods, but in a building of some kind with smooth metal walls. There were a lot of screens around, glass and see-through. Men and women sat at consoles, all of them looking at her.

"Vallah, you're aboard the Asgard rescue ship Endeavor. And your sister doesn't recognize you because you look...different. Our transporter and molecularizer reassembled you with your base DNA, stripping out the junk DNA that was in your body. Well, that and any foreign objects such as clothing, jewelry, and other...markings." The man speaking was large, standing almost two feet taller than her, which had to be impossible. Eight-foot-tall men didn't exist. He had long light brown hair that flowed over his shoulders. The top had been pulled out of his face and was secured behind his head, which showed ears that tipped into a point. He...was beautiful.

"I'm sorry, what did you say? What's an Asgard?" She had to buy some time while she took in her surroundings.

He smiled. "I'm an Asgard. So are the other people in this room, including you. Would you please allow our nurse to hand you a robe?"

Covering her naked body had been secondary to keeping herself safe. Since no one seemed to be rushing her, she agreed. "Okay, but only her. Everyone else, stay back."

The laughter he tried to stifle gave her a start. "Of course."

She glared at him while the woman handed her a soft dark brown robe. She slipped it on, securing it with a fabric belt the woman handed her, tying it tight.

"What's this about DNA?" She looked back at the man who had spoken to her.

"When Valerie had her embryo placed, we added the junk DNA—what we used to make the human race—so that you would blend. The molecularizer removed it and you now are 100 percent Asgard. Here." He waved his hand over a screen, and an image of a woman was displayed. She had long chestnut hair and ears that went up to a point like the man who was speaking. Vallah waved her hand and so did the woman on the screen. It was…it was her reflection.

"You said this was a ship?"

"Yes, a spaceship. You're in the stars now. Your planet is about to be destroyed. We saved as many as we could."

"Wait. Just…" She held up her hand and closed her eyes. She just could not wrap her head around what he was telling her. "Who are you?"

"We are Asgards, the original creators of the human race."

"No, let's start a bit smaller. Who are *you*? What's your name?" The whole room stared at her as if waiting for a bomb to explode.

His smile widened and he bowed. "I am Thor. It's very nice to finally meet you, Vallah. And you, Vallah Sigrid, were named after our heaven for warriors, Valhalla."

With a huff, she rolled her eyes. "And you would know this…how?"

"My father named you."

There was no way in the world this alien knew her or her mother. This had to be some elaborate trick by Snow, complete with a beautiful giant with a dashing smile. He was trying to woo her, to trick her.

"Right." She lifted a brow. *Nice try, asshole. I'm not quite that naive.*

"Vallah, the important thing is this. You need to understand that in about three to five minutes, your planet, will be destroyed. I know it will be difficult to watch, but with our long-range scanners, we can view it, if you wish. You are...a person of interest to our people. It's important that you are completely aware of what's going on. Do you wish to see this event?"

If they were going to stick with this cover story, then she was interested to see how far this elaborate plan went. "My sister?"

Thor bowed at the waist. "We can drop her off in the medical wing so she can be looked after until she can accept what is happening. No harm will come to her, you have my word."

"Well, Thor of the Asgards, know that if you break your word, I'll break your legs. I'll *start* there, anyway."

He stepped closer to her until he was only a foot away. She stood her ground as he crossed his arms over his chest and looked down on her. His arms were large and lean. He did not seem to take her threat seriously. "So, the sister that betrayed you and your family is worth a scuffle with someone who just saved you from impending doom?"

"She's still my sister." To make her point, she stepped closer to him, tilting her head up to look him eye to eye. "And yes, I would kill for her still."

"You have a pure heart, Vallah, even if you think you're dead inside. Come, we're running out of time."

How does he know that?

With that, he spun on his heel and charged down a hall, opening doors with a wave of his hand. They seemed to disappear into the walls before closing once more behind them.

The man carrying her sister placed her on a bed in the medical wing and covered her with a blanket. Satisfied that she was okay, Vallah looked to Thor. "Okay, now what?"

He turned and began walking down another corridor. She followed him from a few steps behind for her own security. He waved his hand one final time, opening a door to a large room with what she could only estimate had about two hundred people standing, looking at a large screen on one wall. The screen showed numerous spacecraft grouped together, all pointing in the same direction.

"What are those?" She asked.

"That's the bulk of the Asgard fleet. As I said, we saved as many worthy humans as we could manage. Those that we thought had hearts black as coal, we left behind. It wasn't an easy decision, but one that took nearly one Midgard year to make."

"What is Midgard?" She wanted to ask how many had been saved and who.

"Earth to you, Midgard to us." He turned to face her, and he placed his hands on her shoulders. She tensed, ready to fight back. "Vallah, please understand the death of a planet is a very big deal to us. We seeded Earth with life. We've watched the humans grow, and for a long time, we had high hopes. When the Centurions came and polluted your bodies with their vaccine, we were too late to stop them. At first, we thought maybe their intentions were pure. Wars had stopped. Humans seemed less inclined to breed themselves to overcrowding. But then, through examination, we found they'd poisoned you. Then…it turned to a very dark planet for the females."

She stared at him, trying to decide if this was all true. Were they really in space? She'd seen technology fool people before.

"So what is going on, then?"

He turned her to face the monitor, keeping both hands

on her shoulders. "We come from the planet Nibiru, which comes in close proximity to Midgard every 3,500 of your years. In your year 1995, we realized the trajectory was getting dangerously close to your planet. We spent the next thousand years monitoring the situation and realized that our worlds would collide on the next cycle. So, we set out to find a planet to relocate our race, and the one we created...the humans. We've spent the last five hundred years preparing that planet to receive you."

The image on the monitor changed. Now a large red planet was getting close to Earth. "Why is it red?"

"It superheated when it passed by your star. There's no life on Nibiru anymore. It just burns. As you can see, a third of your planet has already been scorched."

It was true. The side of Earth that faced the burning planet was black, and the darkness was spreading. The images were zoomed in and flipped from around the world. Debris floated everywhere as the gravitational pull of both planets combined. People, bodies, cars...everything. Then the image changed again and the whole of Earth was on fire.

It wasn't until she felt Thor's grip on her shoulders that she realized she was shaking.

"I'm very sorry, Vallah."

William...he was a decent man. Had he been saved? What about her Amazons?

Both planets were now breaking apart as they collided. The screen went black before it came back up again. "Our long-range scanners are now our only mode of viewing. We only have a few more minutes to watch before we must leave. We're five light years away, but the radiation levels will be more than what our shields can handle."

She could never go home. Never again. It was gone.

Sobs and screams filled the room as humans watched their home destroyed. They were all now refugees, at the mercy of these Asgard people. She could only hope their motives were pure.

"I've seen enough." She looked down at her hand, the marital mark gone. They hadn't lied about that. She was whole, but...a whole different Vallah. Her brain went numb.

"I'll show you to your living quarters. We have to travel 600 light years to get to the new planet, giving you plenty of time to rest." As he steered her by her shoulders, she simply complied. If she was really aboard a spaceship, where could she really go?

"Vallah?"

She hadn't realized she was already in her room. "Hmm?"

"I said I'll leave you now." Thor stood with his brow furrowed.

"No." She grabbed his arm. It was strong and warm. "I'd like some clothing, and I'd like to come with you. I'm not prepared to sit in a room alone right now." She could get more information with him than by herself.

"That's not a good idea. I have many responsibilities, and you'll become fatigued, especially after everything you've just been through." He placed his hand on hers.

She wasn't going to take no for an answer. "Clothes?"

"Pure Asgard stubbornness. Fine." He went to a control panel and pressed a few buttons. "Vallah Sigrid," he spoke aloud. A door to his left opened, and clothing that looked just like what she'd been wearing hung in view. "I'll go in the hall while you change." Without waiting for any response, Thor stepped outside.

She didn't want him to change his mind and leave her there, so she snagged her clothing from the closet and slid it on as quickly as she could. Fully clothed and feeling more confident, she stood at the door. "How do I open this stupid thing?"

Thor had waved his hands to open doors. Unless he had some sort of supernatural powers, maybe it was just sensors that picked up motion. Vallah waved her hand, and the doors parted down the middle. Thor stood, leaning against the wall in the hallway.

"That was fast. I see you're using your DNA to your advantage already." He smirked at her. "Here," he said, handing her a small yellow cube, "if you insist on not resting, then you must eat this to keep up your strength."

"What in the hell is that?" No way was she going to be drugged again. "I think I'll wait. Thank you."

"Unacceptable. This is a nutritional supplement. It's small and compact, making it easier to nourish an entire fleet of starships full of refugees. Having your body de-molecularized and then re-molecularized removes any nutritional storages in your stomach. You're going to be fatigued, and I have a lot to accomplish before arriving at the new planet. So, you need to keep up. Eat it, or stay in your room." He stood holding the cube in his hand.

She wanted to fight, to argue, to avoid eating anything unfamiliar. Not knowing how long the journey would take and remembering that she hadn't eaten since her dinner with William, she relented and took the cube. When she popped it in her mouth, an explosion of flavor erupted on in her mouth. Strawberries and cream, with a hint of something fresh, like mint, danced on her palate.

"These blue portals are where you can find a drink," he explained. He slid open a small blue door and pulled out an odd-looking clear, gelatinous object in the shape of a cylinder. "It's condensed water. Just put it in your mouth."

"Condensed water?"

He released a big sigh. "Look, I know this is all new, but I don't have time to explain everything. I just saved your life, so you're going to have to display a modicum of trust."

Trust for complete strangers was outside Vallah's wheelhouse of experience. He was right; he'd just rescued her and a ton of other humans. With a shrug, she put the small cylinder in her mouth and swallowed. The first thing she noticed was that she felt full...fuller than she had her entire life. Her mouth was wet and she felt no thirst.

"Follow," he said over his shoulder as he headed down the hall.

Vallah had to walk twice as fast as normal to keep up with his long strides.

"We manufacture condensed water for the same reason we manufacture the cubes. It's smaller and takes up less room on the ship. The water has entered your stomach and expanded, causing the cube to expand. That is why you feel full." With a wave of his hand, another set of doors to his left opened.

A tall Asgard woman with white hair quickly approached with a glass screen in her hand. "Commander Thor, you're needed in Medical Unit 3B."

He nodded, turned, and headed down another hall. Vallah was already regretting her decision to accompany him. They walked for nearly five minutes when he came to a halt. He turned and faced her. "I wanted to wait until our medical team had her put back together. But...behind this door is something that will most likely be upsetting to you. Are you absolutely certain you can handle that?"

"What is it? My sister?"

"No. Your sister is sleeping. But you did not answer my question." The two feet he had on her was beginning to give her a stiff neck. Her Amazon women were always a bit taller than her, but not so tall she had to tilt her head up.

She crossed her arms over her chest. "I was in the middle of rescuing my sister when you snatched me up. I came to in my birthday suit and, within a few minutes, watched my home planet get completely decimated. I haven't gone insane yet, so whatever is behind that door, I'm most certain it isn't going to knock the wind out of me. Just open the damned door already."

Thor's brows shot toward his hairline. For an alien, his surprise mimicked a human's very closely. "Very well."

When the door opened, Vallah realized how very wrong she was. A thin, frail woman sat in an exam chair, reclined back with a device wrapped around her head. What Vallah could only assume was an Asgard doctor stood beside her looking at a small glass screen.

"Commander Thor, she's been asking for you."

The frail woman in the chair looked so much like Valerie Sigrid she could have been her twin, except for the darker skin and elongated ears.

"Vallah," the woman gasped. Her bony hand lifted in the air.

"Mother?" Tears stung her eyes as she tried to understand in that split second what was unfolding. Was her mother alive? Was she really an alien too? Was Vallah actually an alien?

The frail creature smiled and stroked her own elongated ear. "Anunaki."

"The device is healing the physical damage, Commander Thor. However, I'm not certain we can reverse years of torture."

"We will do everything we can. Correct?" Thor looked over his shoulder at Vallah.

Vallah locked eyes with him. "Is this really my mother?"

He nodded.

Her knees buckled as she fell to her mother's feet. "Momma," she whispered. "You're alive."

She reached out, stroking Vallah's ear. "Anunaki," she said again.

Thor took a knee. "Valerie, we are going to give you the best care in our power. Vallah is safe. Your human daughter is safe. Rest." He bowed his head to her, then stood to his feet. "Come, Vallah, if you're going to refuse to rest, then we must go."

She could not make her feet move. Ten years' worth of pent-up emotion came bubbling to the surface. A loud sob escaped her as she plummeted her face into her mother's lap. Once more, she felt like the frightened eleven-year-old girl, terrified to leave her mother's side.

A cool, bony hand swept loose hairs off Vallah's face. "Anunaki. Strong." Her mother's gibberish wasn't making any sense.

Vallah wiped her eyes. "I'm going to let the doctor take care of you now. But I'll be back."

Thor put his hand on her shoulder. "That's very wise." He stepped to the side and tapped on a transparent glass screen.

"Commander Thor, how may I be of assistance?" a male voice came over a speaker.

"Asmund, please take over for the next hour."

"Understood."

Thor turned to Vallah. "Come."

She felt as if she were trying to lift not only her own body weight, but that of a boar as she stood. She followed him down a few corridors until they reached a small room. He motioned for her to sit.

"Will she be okay?" she croaked.

"I certainly hope so. Your mother is Asgard. Every Asgard life matters to us. But lay your mind to rest. She will have the absolute best care when we reach the new Midgard." He sat across from her. "Are you okay?"

She shook her head no, but said, "Yeah."

"Look at me," he said with a tone soft as satin. When she looked at him, he smiled. "Are you okay?" he repeated.

"Physically, I think I'm fine. I just couldn't understand the words my mother used."

"Anunaki?" he asked.

"Yeah, what the hell is that supposed to mean?"

"Over time, we've been known by many names. Your mother's people stayed on Earth long after most of us left. They became known as the Anunaki in Sumeria. Some call us by our proper names, the Asgard." He leaned against the table. "I guess I should start from the beginning?"

She looked at him, bewilderment weighing her down. "Sure."

"When we came to your planet the first time, it was

crawling with life, but none of it really cognizant. The Cro-Magnon man, dinosaurs…various other wildlife. So we began a settlement. But there were so few of us, and we needed manual labor. The Cro-Magnons were just untrainable. So we began looking at alternatives. We combined some of their DNA with ours and made humans. Humans were the middle ground. They learned quickly. They were eager to please, and they worshipped us for what they thought were magical powers. It was really just advanced technology."

"So everyone is Asgard, or has some Asgard in them?"

He shook his head. "No, we let evolution take place after that. The human genome advanced on its own, which is why your anthropologists never really put it together. Eventually, the theory of the ancient alien came about. That's when we really stopped returning to Earth. We didn't want to confirm their suspicions."

This made no sense to her. She leaned in toward him. "Why the hell not? It was the truth."

He huffed. "You don't even know why we left." Thor leaned back in his chair, as if he was trying to be more relaxed. "We had the best of intentions initially. However, the Asgards of old were not without their flaws. A few relished their god-like status and really played into it. Some were very good to the humans; others were the worst kind of ruler you can imagine. After several generations, it was decided by the collective that we leave the humans to evolve on their own. We had interfered enough. Gone would be the rulers and other supposed gods. We thought time would teach the humans that we were not gods, just an advanced race. We left clues, but very few. The human race would have to advance in science and technology to get the truth." He shook his head. "They never really figured it out. Those that had the most accurate theories were laughed out of the human science community. It was the best cover-up the Asgards could have hoped for."

Vallah tried to wrap her head around what he was

saying. "Okay, then where the hell did the Centurions come from?"

"Do you remember the old stories about little grey aliens?" Thor laughed. "Oh yes, we did receive Earth's television stations through long-range sensors. My favorite television show is still The Flintstones." He laughed to himself for a moment. "Anyway, an alien craft crashed on Earth and was spirited away by the government. Later, film was released, as well as many claims of alien interactions."

"What? I thought that was a hoax. At least, that's what the history books indicated."

"No, the Centurion race had decayed over time. They began coming to Earth to take human women and steal their eggs. They began crossing their DNA with the DNA we created. It took some time, but eventually, they were able to reinvigorate themselves. There are a few really old greys left, but for the most part, they look totally human."

Vallah closed her eyes and tried to recall the films she'd seen when she was young about the Centurion visit. "But they don't look entirely human. They have weird-shaped heads and that odd cleft on their forehead."

Thor nodded. "They're not as good at DNA manipulation as we are. They do look odd." Again, he smiled. "I think that's why they despise us."

Fatigue began to weigh heavy on her. Her legs ached, and the throbbing was beginning in her arms. "I really don't understand. Why eradicate the human race when you need us to provide viable eggs?"

"They don't need the eggs anymore. The Centurion are all now half-breeds and no longer need the human DNA we created."

"Wait...so they're part Asgard, too. Right?"

"Yes, but they don't know that. There is very little Asgard DNA left in the human race, so I doubt there is any more than a trace in any given Centurion." Leaning forward, he placed his hands on the table. "The point of me telling you this is to tell you that we left a few elders behind. They stayed and carried on a small but effective group of our kind. We had to make them blend, and blend they did. Your mother's ancestors have been training their daughters in the old ways for a very, very long time. We protected our Asgard daughters the best we knew how. And this…this is why you had no idea your mother was not who you thought she was. She not only held the Asgard tradition, our secrets, but our bloodline. She is an exceptional warrior, Vallah."

"I can't. I just can't take any more right now. My head is…it's full. My mother and my sister…they will be taken care of?" She wasn't asking, but she was looking for reassurance.

"They'll get the best care we have to offer. I give you my word, and to me, that is everything." He stood from his chair. "One last thing…"

She couldn't imagine trying to cope with one more thing at the moment. She needed a moment to herself to think. She regretted not staying in her room like he'd asked in the first place. "Go on."

He placed his hand on her shoulder. "Your legs and arms are sore because your body is expanding. Your bones are restructuring to your Asgard DNA. There's a small box next to the bed in your room. Inside it is pain relief, should you need it."

"Seriously? I'm going to grow another two feet?" She shook her head. "Anything else, or can I go to my room?"

"No, you probably won't gain that much height. Perhaps a foot, maybe more. I'll take you to your room."

The short walk back to her room happened almost without her awareness. She sat on the edge of the bed, until the door closed behind Thor. She fell back on the bed, then swung her legs over, which were really beginning to ache. She hadn't been this uncomfortable since she'd started training with the Amazons.

She wasn't human, and neither was her mother, but her sister was not the same alien race. Her planet had been destroyed, and she had no idea who was left. Her masters had had her study science, but she didn't have the faintest of ideas how far away a light year was, nor how long it would take to travel 600 of them.

What now? What would life be? Who would be in it? Would there be any point?

CHAPTER SEVEN

"Vallah, ma'am, please wake up."

Vallah bolted upright and stared at the tall woman in the white coat staring down at her.

"Hello. I'm the ship's physician. May I examine you?"

"I'm fine." That was a lie. Her head throbbed, as did her extremities. Why couldn't this woman just let her rest?

The woman's blue eyes squinted as she smiled. Her silken hair cascaded in a thick braid that reminded Vallah of her Amazon masters. "I doubt that very much. Please allow me to examine you."

"Fine."

The woman looked into her eyes and ears before pointing a device at her that whistled and beeped. "You're in a great deal of discomfort. Your molecules have settled in nicely, but the transformation has caused your energy stores to be depleted." She walked across the room and pressed a few buttons on a panel. A coffee mug appeared with steam rising from the top. She carried it back to Vallah. "Drink this."

"What is it?" she asked as she eyed the mug.

"It's medicinal tea."

Vallah took the mug. "Thank you." After a quick sniff,

she took a sip and found it to be pleasant and velvety.

"It took my arms and legs about three days to feel normal. I suspect it'll be the same for you." She smiled and tapped on the screen in her hand. "Otherwise, you're in optimal health."

"Wait…you've been transformed before?" Finally! Someone who might understand how confusing the situation might be.

"May I sit?" With a nod from Vallah, the doctor pulled a small stool out of a cupboard. "I spent three years on Earth studying Earth medicine and cultures so as to better understand their kind. I had to blend in, so I went through it twice. Growing is easier than shrinking, I can assure you. But if I can give you a bit of advice?"

"Yes, yes please. I'm so overwhelmed and just…confused." Admitting that wasn't easy for her, but there was little left in the way of grace.

"Human culture is very different from ours. When you go to your new home, keep an open mind. Many of the cultural norms are…opposite. We Asgards are a free and loving society, but can be evasive or very forward. Humans are a bit more…reserved about things. Just remain open-minded, and try not to get too frustrated as you learn our ways."

"Where are my manners?" Vallah smoothed her hand on her pants. "I don't even know your name."

"Judith," she said with a smile.

"It's very nice to meet you. Whoa." Valla grabbed the bed. "I don't feel…I feel dizzy."

"Ah yes, you're about to take a very long nap. That's the tea. You shouldn't feel any more pain until you wake, and then it should be minimal." She scooped the cup out of Vallah's hand and helped her lie back. "Rest now, Vallah. When you wake, we'll be home."

****

Vallah walked through a plush garden of mysterious flowers and thick, furry bush. When she ran her fingers along the fur of the bush, it shimmered in the light from above.

"I'm dreaming." It was clear to her that this was not reality. She tried to rouse herself, to no avail. "Guess I'll explore."

Looking down, she noticed her bare feet in the middle of a moss pathway that snaked through the foliage. She could feel the fibers of the moss tickle her feet as she made her way. With a deep breath in, she smelled the perfume of the alien flower garden. *I've never seen these species of plant before.*

"My Bella," a phantom breath blew past her ear.

"Seth?" Looking around, she couldn't see anyone else. *Must be part of this dream.*

A dark spot appeared in the middle of the trail. As she walked closer, she noticed it was a small house. It was rustic, with a stucco exterior and wood plank roof. The edges of the air surrounding the house were blurry, watery. It was if her dream were a moving painting. When she approached the door, it opened for her.

A fire burned in a small fireplace on the wall opposite her. She could hear the crackle of the logs and smell the faint hint of smoke in the air.

"Welcome home," Thor said, seemingly appearing out of thin air.

Her heart raced, and she turned to follow the sound of his voice. He was lying naked on a makeshift bed on the floor.

"Come to me."

Almost in an instant, she was naked and next to him, her fingers wound in his hair.

Time was skipping...maybe it was the dream. His face was between her legs. Her body was ablaze as he licked and nipped at her clit.

Every cell in her felt like it would explode as she

became dizzy with pleasure. She felt hot, like she might combust.

He settled between her legs, pausing. His lips crushed into hers. A small whine of need made its way from her mouth to his when he finally entered her. A vast explosion of color surrounded them when he entered her. She cried out, begging for more.

Suddenly, she was on her stomach, Thor behind her. His hand snaked under her chest, over her throat, until he was cupping her chin as he drove into her from behind. He held her firm as he picked up the pace.

****

"Vallah, we have arrived."

She opened her eyes to see Thor gently shaking her.

"Huh?" She sat up and rubbed her eyes. "What?"

"We're at the new Midgard. It's time to get off the ship, and I'm happy to say I have a pleasant surprise for you." He held out his hand.

She let him help her up. When she got to her feet, she immediately recognized that he was now only a mere four inches taller than she. She'd really gained some size as she slept, though her clothes didn't feel too small.

At that moment, her dream came to the front of her mind, and she could feel the heat in her face as arousal oozed out of her.

"Whoa, Vallah. What is that about?" Thor laughed.

"What?"

He shook his head. "I can smell it on you—the arousal."

"Nothing but the remnants of a dream, but thank you for bringing it up." She tried to brush it off, but his words only served to embarrass her further. He seemed to take note. *Smelled my arousal? What the hell?*

"Come, some of your friends are waiting for you."

She wanted to ask what he meant, but he was already

on the move. She'd have to learn to adjust if she was going to keep up with a man who was always moving in the opposite direction. The corridors were full of humans moving to the other end of the ship. If they were getting off the ship, why weren't they following the others?

When they turned down another corridor, Vallah could feel a fresh breeze blowing, and could smell the gentle fragrance of a nearby garden. Wherever they were, flowers were in bloom. Sunshine illuminated a lush green surface as they walked down a long ramp. When her feet finally met with the ground, she looked up to discover a breathtaking view. A waterfall spilled into a lagoon that was surrounded by lush greenery and tropical flowers.

After a deep breath in through her nose, she let it go. "This is heaven."

"This is home," Thor whispered in her ear. She'd nearly forgotten they were together.

"I think I can live with that."

"Vallah!" A familiar voice caught her attention. She turned to find Tatiana and Katana moving their way.

She fell to her knees. "You're alive!"

"Get off the ground. You're a warrior, damn it. At least I trained you to be a warrior." Tatiana held out her hand and gave her a lift off the ground. "I barely recognized you. Asgard looks good on you!"

Vallah immediately noticed Tatiana had to look up to her. That was a first. She threw her arms around the women and pulled them in close. "I'm so thankful you're alive."

Katana patted her on the back. "Of course, we've been here the whole time."

"What?" She pulled back. "Here?"

"Yes, you've returned to Midgard the Second." She beamed at Vallah. "The transporter brought you here, to us. Let me tell you, it was hell trying to keep you strictly in our village."

"You really have to come up with a better name for

this planet," Tatiana said to Thor.

He shook his head. "We've been a bit preoccupied."

Tatiana's red hair was loosely tied behind her back. Loose tendrils floated in the breeze. "You must be starving. Come, let's go home."

"Home…" The sudden realization that Vallah had no idea about the living situation caused her to visually search the area. "What does that mean, exactly?"

Nadia winked. "Well, you're going to stay with Thor and his…well, your people, but we're in the neighboring village, just a ten-minute walk. Maybe five with those new long legs of yours. A feast has been prepared in honor of your return—well, in celebration of the rescue of the human race and the return of our Asgard brothers and sisters."

"But"—she looked to Thor— "what about my mother and sister?"

"Your mother is staying in the hospital for a few more days. She has made great progress, but she needs to heal. Your sister has been sedated off and on. She's going to spend some time with one of your human psychologists to determine if she's mentally stable. Then, we'll decide where she goes from there." He shifted his weight from one foot to the other, which she found odd. Why did he look nervous?

Nadia took her hand. "Vallah, your mother is one of us. Well, she's Asgard and Amazon. She will have a home wherever she chooses. I realize you have been through quite the ordeal. You're probably exhausted and hungry. Let us go to the Asgard side of the planet."

"Asgard side?"

The more information she received, the more questions she had.

"Yes, well, we, uh…we have different customs from the humans, so we constructed our own domiciles on the other side of the planet. Several Asgards will remain here to assist the humans in their settlements. But we thought it best to keep our cultures separate for now." He cleared his throat. "Let's get moving. The others are waiting."

More nervousness. What was going on? This advanced alien was the commander of his own ship. Why, all of the sudden, did he seem like a nervous teenager? Vallah would have to get to the bottom of that barrel later.

She walked with the group to a small, square stone building. Inside was a vertical stone circle that looked about ten feet in diameter. A squat pedestal of metal with a slanted glass top was erected to the side. Oval-shaped glass objects rested on the larger slanted piece of glass. Markings Vallah did not recognize were etched into the top.

"What is this?"

Tatiana began pointing at the glass. "It's a stargate. Usually they're used to hop from planet to planet. But this was constructed to cut through to the other side of this planet for ease of travel. Well, depending on where the stones are moved, you'll wind up at a different location."

"Oh, like the casket?"

"Casket?" The look of horror on Thor's face made her smile.

"I was just a child when I stepped into it. It looked like a glass casket to me." Vallah shrugged.

"Asgard beaming technology," he chuckled. "It transported you from there to an open gate, which brought you here."

"Uh, okay?"

"Don't worry"—Nadia nudged her in the ribs as she began moving the small glass objects— "you'll catch on."

When she moved the final object, the stone circle hummed loudly, then a small explosion of water shot from the front.

"Never stand in front of a forming event horizon. It will incinerate you," Nadia instructed as she walked toward the stone circle. The water calmed and now stood vertically as if a pool encased in the stone circle.

The two Amazon women stepped through. Vallah

looked at Thor. "Uh, you first."

A soft smile spread across his lips. He took her hand. "We'll do it together. It's totally pain free, I assure you."

His hand felt strong and warm as it closed around hers. She walked up to the shimmering circle and touched the surface. It reacted just like a pool of water.

When he stepped through, he pulled her with him. The pull was a bit harsh. She felt like Jell-O being sucked through a vacuum when, nearly instantaneously, she stepped out of the pool, completely dry, in a much larger building.

"That was wild. Where are we?" Vallah released Thor's hand.

"Just outside the Hall. This is where we hold meetings and social gatherings."

She paused for a moment, taking in the scene of what looked like the tropics. A dirt path lead down thick foliage that butted up against a thick forest. Wildflowers dotted the tall grass, adding a heavenly fragrance to the air.

With a tug on her wrist, Thor urged her to move forward.

The hall was enormous. Ten long tables were lined with roasted meats, fruit, vegetables, and other items Vallah didn't recognize. Desserts maybe? Large pots containing soups steamed on one heavy stone table.

Thor stood a little straighter. "I realize there are a lot of people in here. Just relax and be yourself. I don't expect you to remember every name."

The group of a couple hundred Asgards and Amazons moved about with plates of food.

"Good, because my memory isn't that good." She smiled and began walking toward the table of food, led by a growling stomach; she'd worry about etiquette later.

"Holy Mother, you look good as an Asgard!"

Vallah smiled when she saw who was speaking. Olivia, her personal educator, approached. Her blonde hair was knotted over her shoulder. Unlike the other Amazon women, she had a much fairer complexion and eyes so blue they almost appeared white.

"It's the ears, right?" she teased.

"Oh yes, the pointy ears are very appealing. It's good to see you well, Vallah. You must sit with us. We've been very worried about you. The others will want to hear of your adventures."

Vallah piled her plate high with various fruits, vegetables, and a steak before following Oliva to a table full of Amazon women. After numerous greetings and hugs, she finally sat and began to eat. They prompted her for war stories, so she filled them in from her return to Earth until her arrival at the new planet.

Tatiana nudged Nadia, who sat next to her. "A certain commander can't take his eyes off our Vallah."

Vallah sat up straight. "Excuse me?"

She followed their line of sight until she saw Thor staring at her. When their eyes locked, his face reddened.

"Busted," Tatiana said with a laugh.

"And you are a bunch of feared warriors?" An Asgard man walked by the table with a large beverage in his hand. "You're acting like a bunch of teenagers."

Nadia winked at Vallah. "You think so, Baldwin? Care to put your theory to a challenge?"

He lifted his mug to his mouth and, after a large gulp of whatever he was drinking, he smiled. "Theory?"

She tossed her thick braid over her shoulder. "I'll bet our Vallah can out throw you. Say…best two out of three times?"

"Never!" He tossed back the rest of his drink and slammed his glass on the table. "That's an easy task. What's the wager?"

"Hang on!" Vallah objected. "Why do I have to be involved?"

"If she wins, I get a week of Asgard combat training. If she loses…then you get to train as an Amazon for the same timeframe."

Every Amazon woman at the table gasped. Vallah began looking around. "What? What's going on?"

Tatiana leaned over and whispered, "An Asgard has never trained an Amazon, and we Amazons never train men...ever."

All that pressure!

"Let me put an end to this right now," Thor said as he approached.

Baldwin straightened his back and looked forward. "Commander Thor, I must apologize."

"Stay out of this, Thor. Baldwin here was just about to make a losing bet."

"Hang on! I was two feet shorter five seconds ago, Nadia. My center of balance is off, and—"

Nadia cut her off with a wave of her hand. Vallah knew there was no discussing anything any further. She slumped in her chair in defeat.

Thor looked at Vallah, pity painted on his face. "Don't do this to her, Nadia. She needs to get her bearings."

Something about his words, about his need to defend her, irritated Vallah.

She shot out of her chair, palms on the table. "Excuse me, but I can speak for myself."

"Deal!" Baldwin nearly shouted his answer.

Seemed Thor didn't have the control he thought he did.

"Let's go!" Tatiana leaped from the table. The others followed suit.

Thor began to walk away. For reasons Vallah could not understand, she didn't want to see him go. "Thor?"

He turned to face her. "Vallah?"

"Don't you want to see who wins?" She smirked. She'd been an expert at throwing knives since she was only thirteen. It was a chance to show her skills, and she didn't want him to miss it.

"You want me there?" he asked.

With a large smile, she gave him a nod. "I could use the

moral support."

When he turned to walk back toward the group, Vallah felt her pulse increase…was her heart racing for a man? For an alien man? Since they were technically the same race, was he really alien? She looked away to clear her thoughts.

The crowd began to move outside.

Tatiana found a tree without any low-hanging branches. She reached in the pouch strapped to her side and pulled out a small tin. Vallah knew the tin well. White paste used for marking. She'd marked so many targets for Nadia to torture Vallah, the image of that tin was burned in her brain.

"Best two out of three," Nadia announced. She looked to Baldwin, who was busy tying back his thick black hair.

"Agreed."

"Ladies," Nadia said to three Amazon women standing nearest to her. "Blades?"

The three women pulled out their knives and handed them over.

"What?" Baldwin protested. "You're going to give her three different-sized knives for this?"

"Of course. Where's the challenge if I give her three identical blades?"

Vallah recalled having various knives having to be thrown at the same target when she was just a teen. It taught her how to gauge her throw well. Having to adjust actually sharpened her skill and made her much more aware of the knife she was wielding.

He shrugged. "It's your bet to lose."

"Or win," she shot back.

Vallah handled the first and largest knife and tossed it between her hands a few times. When she was confident that she had the balance figured, she aimed, leaned back, and threw. It hit the target dead center.

Happily, she stepped aside to see what he had to answer with.

He tilted his head to one side, then the other, stretching his neck before tossing his dark ponytail over his shoulder.

"Today, Baldwin," Nadia teased.

With a swift movement, he lifted the knife over his shoulder, pointed with his other hand, then launched it toward the target. It hit the butt of Vallah's first throw and hit the target at the outer rim.

Thor sighed.

"What's wrong?" Vallah asked. "Embarrassed?"

The corner of his mouth turned up as he fought to hide his smirk. "Hardly. I'd actually like to see you win, but then I have to watch my man humiliated. Sort of a lose-lose situation. Looks like you're up."

She stepped forward. The next knife was lighter and would be more difficult to lodge in the hardwood. She flipped it in her hand a few times to gauge the weight. Taking aim, she noticed Baldwin staring at her hard. She fought a laugh before launching the knife. It wedged next to her first bullseye."

"Damn," he groaned.

After a few cheers from her Amazons, she reclaimed her spot next to Thor.

"Very impressive," he said with a smile. "Remind me not to anger you if you have a knife in your possession. I fear my lieutenant has lost already."

Vallah patted him on the shoulder. "I'll let you in on a secret. He lost after my first throw."

His brows rose. "A little overly confident, aren't we?"

With a shake of her head, she let out a small giggle. "It's a strategic part of the bet. I'm guessing the Asgards are a bit…chivalrous toward women?"

He gave an affirmative nod.

"If I managed to get the largest knife even close to the target, his knife has no chance of getting close because the first knife is in the way. I'm pretty good with knives because Nadia made me throw them for hours a day until I could do it blindfolded. She knew I'd get close, if not right on target. She was betting I'd win before he even agreed to the bet."

"Scandalous. I had no idea the Amazons were so shifty." He smiled at Nadia, who was watching them, before he nodded in her direction. "So she wanted some Asgard training?"

"It's more likely she wants to beat the shit out of him, then bed him down. They have an insatiable sexual appetite."

As suspected, Baldwin's second throw wasn't even close. The game was over; Vallah won without even having to throw the third knife.

"Let's keep this discussion between the two of us, huh?"

"Done. Now, would you like to go to the settlement and see your surroundings?"

The crowd began to dissipate after Vallah's win. She stood looking at Thor. Images of her dream began dancing in the back of her mind. Now that she was closer to his size, he wasn't as intimidating as before. His broad, lean shoulders rippled with strength underneath, and his thick, muscular arms swayed as he walked. She wondered how accurate her dream was with regard to his physique unclothed.

A light rain began to fall, making the already hot and humid air a bit thicker.

"Have to love the tropical weather here." Thor smiled as they headed down the path away from the meeting hall.

Vallah laughed. "I was hoping for a bath, but this isn't what I had in mind."

"Well, we have a very nice bath at the house. There's a small lagoon in back that's nice for swimming as well. I suspect it a hot spring, because it's always very warm and there are no fish. But it's almost as nice as a bath. When my muscles are sore, I'll stretch out in the lagoon."

"Wow," Vallah gasped as she looked around, "this place grows in beauty every moment that I'm here. I almost hate to disturb the place with our presence." There was a small waterfall off to her left that spilled into a small lagoon. Large birds swooped in and out of the falling water as they sang. A pair of swans floated on the lagoon's edge. A few feet away were the largest tiger lilies Vallah had ever seen.

"Oh, I'll grant you that. It has been a welcomed change to the star city. They did a decent job making you feel like you were in nature, but I just felt closed in there."

"Star city?" She shook her head. "I swear it will take me a lifetime to catch up."

He put his arm around her shoulder. It shocked her at first, but she found it actually eased the tension she was feeling. "Oh, I'm sorry," he apologized, "we're not as, uh, objectionable to physical contact as humans. This must feel odd."

"On the contrary, it's sort of nice. I've been alone for a long time. Receiving the warm embraces from my masters has taken the edge off, and while it did startle me at first, it was nice." She felt the heat rising up her cheeks.

He replaced his arm and they continued to walk. "I'll take you to see the star city if you want. It was originally our settlement while we prepared this planet for habitation. Now it's sort of a meeting place and trading post for other races. It'll be good for you to meet other species and come up to speed with our reality."

"How many alien races are there?" She felt ill. How could they have left the humans in the dark for so long? The human race was always trying to explore space...to see if they were alone.

"Hundreds, though only a dozen or so in this quadrant of the galaxy." He gave her a squeeze. "Don't worry, the Asgards protect their own. We will do our level best to educate you as fast as possible. We won't keep the humans ignorant any longer, though we will tell them the truth a bit more slowly. Humans are prone to panic, and they've been through something very traumatic already."

"Thor, I don't know what your plans are for me, but I'd very much like to visit my mother tomorrow. I haven't seen her in a decade and I thought…I thought…"

"She was dead?" He looked at her as he helped her finish. "She was close, but thankfully we found her in time. The building they had her in had thick walls of concrete and steel. It really messed with our scanners. The underground was easy; the material was all organic."

"The underground? You found them!" She stopped in her tracks. "Maybe you have William and his sister. Maybe they made it!" She put her hands over her mouth. "Oh my God!"

"Who is William?"

"My husband, well, sort of."

"I'm sorry…" He closed his eyes and took a deep breath. "Your husband?"

"Relax. He's not really my husband. It was just a cover story, but I did have his ring imbedded in my flesh for a day, so…" Was that jealousy on his face?

"So you're *not* married?"

Vallah wanted to crack up laughing, but the look of desperation on his face made her quash it. "Geeze, you just met me. Relax. No, I'm not married, *sir*." *You have one sex dream about a guy and he gets all possessive!*

He shook his head. "I must apologize. It's just…there are no Asgard-to-human marriages, and while this might be a culture shock for you, I can assure you, that would be very odd for my people…our people."

"They've been my people for two seconds, Thor. Give me just a few to meet them before I concern myself with their comfort level—or yours, for that matter." She looked at her feet, her boots nearly covered by the hairs of the moss on which she stood. "I was a human until you pulled me onto that ship. It will take me awhile to come to terms with the fact that I'm not anymore."

"Again," he said with a large sigh, "I owe you an apology. It's been a very stressful mission, and I fear my fatigue might be making me cranky. Let's get back to the house so I can grab some whiskey and unwind."

A large hawk circled above them. She watched him soar for a moment before she spotted a bald eagle perched in a tree. "Are all of these Earth transplants?"

"There are some from Earth and some from Nibiru. I should warn you, our cats are very large, almost the size of Earth's cheetah. They act a bit more like loyal dogs, though, and they're needy and demanding of affection. We have one that has adopted us at the house. She thinks she owns me."

As they approached a thick forest, Vallah noted that the trees were enormous. They were the thickest and tallest trees she'd ever seen. She doubted any storm could knock them over. They were as wide as a parking lot and as tall as a skyscraper. As they walked closer, she noticed the largest tree in view had…could it be windows?

"Is that a house or a tree?"

"Both," he said with a smile. "And it's ours."

When they reached the tree, she found three steps made of roots that led to a door. When he opened the door, she gasped. Inside, she could see that the residence was literally carved right into the tree. The furniture, too. It was if the Asgards became one with the tree.

"This is magnificent!" She stepped inside.

"You must be Vallah," a female voice from her left spoke. She turned to see what she could only describe as an albino Asgard, but the woman's beauty was astonishing. Her hair was so blonde it was nearly white. Her eyes, so crystal blue they almost looked white as well.

"Marika, this is Vallah. Vallah, this is Marika."

Marika opened her arms. Reluctantly, Vallah stepped into her embrace. "Welcome, sister. If there is anything you desire, you only need ask." She kissed her on the cheek.

"That's a hell of a welcome," Vallah said as she stepped back. "But I'm willing to take you up on your offer."

Marika smiled and nodded. "What can we do for you?"

"Coffee, and a bath at the earliest possible convenience. Please."

"Coffee?" The moment Marika asked, Vallah moaned. Did the Asgards not believe in coffee?

"Caife," Thor interjected.

Marika drew her hands together in front of her chest. "Ah, caife! Or coffee, as you said. I'll have it for you by the time Thor finishes the tour!"

The tour proved to be awe-inspiring. The tree was a maze of small rooms and bedrooms. A kitchen and what would be considered a living room resided on the main floor. It was if the Asgards were ants living within the tree, but the furniture seemed to grow from the interior of the tree itself. Even the bed was part of the tree, save for the bedding itself.

"This is amazing. How long did it take to carve out?"

"We never carve into a tree, Vallah. Though our technology has improved, we can communicate with nature, and if we make a request and take care of the planet, it takes care of us. We simply let what you would call Mother Earth know what we need and she provides. In turn, we never take more than we need and we always repair the damage."

"Repair the damage?" She shook her head. "Do I even need to ask?"

"If we harvest something, we replant. If we kill an animal for its flesh, we leave an offering for the forest. We might need room to live, but we never destroy the planet to get it. It's like...a connection and mutual respect. If a tree is diseased, we remove the infected part so the tree can thrive. We only burn wood that is already dead...that sort of thing. Then the ashes are spread so the forest can gain back the carbon and minerals."

She stood in the living quarters, gazing at the furniture...the furniture that had grown into place.

"This is your room." He cleared his throat. "We, uh,

we will get you some clothing. Marika can assist you in that regard."

Thor looked uncomfortable again. She wasn't entirely sure why he kept acting like a shy adolescent, but didn't think it was the time to address his behavior. "This is really incredible."

"The bath is through that door." He walked over and opened it. Light filtered through tiny angled windows. The tub looked as if it were made of a clear stone. "Just pull the chain until the tub is at the desired level, and then pull it again to turn the water off. It's very warm."

She saw a small bag of stones in a mesh bag resting on the side. "What's with the rocks?"

"That's what we use to clean our bodies. We don't use chemicals like on Earth. You'll find a pleasant aroma is released when you dip it in the warm water. The water here is pure, so you'll not need anything else to cleanse your hair."

Vallah had dealt with that when she'd lived with the Amazons. They'd bathed in lagoons and hot springs, never using anything more than natural resources. She wasn't all that surprised, but it was a far cry from the perfumed assault she'd experienced at William's.

With the tour over, he led her back to the main area, where Marika handed her a piping-hot cup of coffee. It was rich and bold, just the way she liked it.

"Go on and have that bath."

"I, uh, should wait until I have some clean clothes to wear. Thor mentioned you might be able to help?" Taking charity was a new experience to her. Other than the help from William and the borrowed clothing, she had not accepted help in a very long time.

"Oh, that's not a problem. Do you like what I'm wearing?"

A loincloth and bra? No. "It's a bit more revealing than I'm used to."

With a smile and a nod, Marika opened a cupboard and

pulled out a small handheld device. "Stand very still." Vallah did as she asked and a blue light scanned the length of her body. "I'll have something suitable on the bed for you when you are done with your bath."

Suitable?

Thor placed his hand between her shoulders. "I have to go. By the time you're cleaned up, the others will be arriving. We'll have our evening meal and you can get to know your people."

The moment he finished his sentence, a large cat tackled him to the floor. Vallah instinctively pulled her knife from its sheath.

"Andromeda!" Thor laughed as the cat licked his face. "Enough! Get off me, you crazy feline!"

Marika and Vallah laughed. Thor had gone from commander of his fleet to this cat's personal pet. That was when Vallah noticed the cat had three sets of legs. One set looked like the front of any other cat. The rear had two sets, though. This was definitely not an Earth-variety cat.

"She's missed you, Commander." Marika wrapped her arms around the cat's shoulders and pulled her back. Thor scrambled to his feet.

"I warned you, Vallah. Her affection is quite aggressive. If I were you, I wouldn't make friends with her. I give her one dead chicken and this is how she has acted ever since." He wiped his face with his shirt. "I'm going while I still have a shred of dignity." He opened the door and left.

Andromeda turned toward Vallah. The cat did something odd. She walked slowly up to Vallah and stood on her back feet, placing her paws gently on Vallah's chest. She was making direct eye contact.

"Uh…what's going on?"

Marika spoke softly, "She's talking to you. Relax your mind and listen."

Vallah could not hear anything, but it was if she received a message from the cat, welcoming her to the family and assuring her she was protected…

"Uh, thank you?"

"You can't say it, Vallah. You must think it."

These people are nuts. Okay, kitty. Thank you.

The cat scoffed. It literally scoffed at her, tilting its head back as if what Vallah thought was offensive. This thing was way too big and powerful to piss off. Just in case it wasn't bullshit...

I'm sorry. My world has been destroyed. I'm just feeling off. Thank you for welcoming me. It was a disjointed and awkward apology, but it was the truth.

The cat seemed to accept and rubbed itself on her as it walked away.

"She's pretty emotional. Gotta watch what you communicate to her." Marika snickered. "Secretly, I think Thor had thoughts that she'd be the only female in his life. That might be why she is so attached...because he needs the companionship."

"What?" Thor a lonely single guy? She didn't believe it.

"Never mind. Go take that bath."

CHAPTER EIGHT

It wasn't until Vallah had begun to relax in the hot water of the bath that a tidal wave of emotions engulfed her. The sheer relief that her mother was still alive was only matched by the disappointment in her sister's actions. It was if she were a complete stranger. Maybe she was. What sort of torment would cause her to turn on her family...to potentially cause her own mother's death?

The planet was gone. So were the pollution, the politics, and the enslavement of women. Would humans desecrate their new world? Could women finally be free?

William, and presumably Karen, had made it out of the underground as well. Her Amazons were never in any danger. There were so many things to be thankful for, yet she agonized over those that didn't make it. Those that might have been worthy of a second chance, but the Asgards just couldn't save everyone.

Asgard...that was who she was now. Born to an Asgard mother, disguised as human, shipped off to the Amazons, then rescued by the Asgards, a race she'd never heard of before but was now a part of. Who was her biological father?

Tears streamed down her face as she finally released all

she'd held inside. For years, she'd held in the tears, unwilling to show the slightest hint of vulnerability. Her mother wanted her to be a warrior, so a warrior she would be. Better a dead warrior than a sex slave to some depraved, entitled asshole.

She had a second chance at life and she wasn't going to waste it. After rinsing her face one final time, she pulled the drain and stepped out of the tub. After a quick drying off with a towel, she stepped into her room to find a pile of clothing on her bed. She dug through, happy to see that in place of loincloths were shorts, pants, and vests. She could be covered if she chose, or reveal a little more on hotter days.

After pulling on a pair of shorts and a matching shirt that was cut like a vest, she slid on a pair of sandals that rested in the bottom of the closet. After managing to get turned around, she finally made it to the main level. There were almost twenty Asgard men and women milling about, talking and eating.

"Vallah." Marika smiled. "I'll let everyone introduce themselves. Everyone, this is Vallah."

The next hour was a blur of handshakes, welcoming hugs, and food. Vallah couldn't recall one single name, just that the Asgards seemed to genuinely welcome her among them. Notable was how little the Asgards wore in terms of clothing. The men were all shirtless, and the women dressed a lot like Marika, wearing loincloths and a bra-like top.

Thor made his entrance, shirtless like the rest. Her eyes immediately traced his torso, impressed with the accuracy of her dream. When he spotted her, he smiled and made his way to her.

"Did you meet everyone?" he asked as he approached.

"Not that I can remember any names, but yes. Does everyone dress so casually all of the time?" She glanced at his abs, silently cursing herself for being so obvious.

"What's wrong? Don't like the view?" He didn't

restrain his laugh this time. Wherever he'd gone, he seemed more relaxed now.

Unwilling to let him think he embarrassed her, she crossed her arms over her chest. "The view is fine. I'm just getting a feel for the culture."

He jutted his chin forward and smirked. "I'm fine? Duly noted."

She couldn't help but laugh at Thor fishing for compliments. "I was wondering…"

He finished for her. "When you can see your family?" When she nodded, he gave a soft smile. "We can go now if you'd like, or we can wait until morning after they've rested. It's your choice. Once you get the hang of using the stargate, you won't need a chaperone."

"I have a feeling there's more than that I need to learn. But I have to tell you, for an advanced race, the Asgards sure choose to live very primitively. It's not really what I expected. I mean, I don't mean any offense, it's just a surprise after being on your ship." *Open mouth, insert foot.*

He put his hand on her back and gently guided her toward the door. "That settles it. We're going to the city." He turned and called out over his shoulder, "We'll be back later."

Guilt punched her square in the abdomen. "I apologize if you feel insulted."

"Insulted? Vallah, we Asgards aren't easy to insult. There was some debate what to do with you once we arrived."

"Debate? Who debated what?" Of all the lives rescued from Earth, there was a debate about her?

"I thought it would be in your best interest to be here with us—to learn our culture so you can adapt more quickly. The Amazons insisted that you have already been stuck with them for far too long without your consent. Marika thought you might want to be with your mother, if we could find her. Farouk wasn't comfortable having you live with us, considering that you might feel more…human than Asgard."

"Farouk?" she asked, trying to recall if she'd met him.

"He's in the city at the moment. Don't worry. He has nothing against you, just…he has trust issues. He doesn't even trust the Nyx, and they've been our allies for centuries."

Nyx…must be another alien race. She felt like any more questions would feel like an inquisition. "So, it seems you won the debate, then. You must be quite convincing."

Thor laughed. "Hardly. It's my rank. My bloodline is very old, which gives me a bit of status. Asgards don't judge status on material possession, rather on the wisdom of the family. Even so, status isn't as important as the collective. It's in our nature to do what we feel is best for everyone…at least, we try."

As they made their way, Vallah noticed a small hut in the middle of a field. It looked suspiciously familiar. "I know this place…" She stopped and stared, trying to figure out how she'd know a small home on an alien planet. "Oh shit."

"What is it? What's wrong?" Thor looked around as if something were about to attack.

"I dreamt of this house while I was on the ship. But how is that possible?" She walked slowly forward. "I've never been here."

"No, you haven't. This is mine. Sometimes the community home is a bit intrusive. I like to be alone, and—did you say you dreamt of my house?" He stared at her as they approached his home. "You're absolutely certain you've seen *this* house?"

"I think so. How else would I have recognized it? Can I go inside?"

He pushed the door open. "Of course."

Vallah was stunned. The fireplace, the bed on the floor—it was exactly as she had dreamed. "Impossible," she gasped.

"So…this is why you were giving off pheromones

when I woke you?" He chuckled.

"Stuff it. Let me just revel in my amazement for a moment." She tried to push back the memories of her dream, but her mind betrayed her. The feel of his hands, the thickness of him inside her—sweat began to form on the back of her neck. "Why are we here?"

"So I can put a shirt on before we go to the city."

She inhaled, smelling the faint odor of a past fire, along with a heady woodsy scent. This place had Thor in every inch of it. Her nipples stiffened under her vest. She could see him pulling a shirt over his head from her peripheral vision, afraid to look him in the face. If he could smell her arousal before, it would be stronger now that she was in his place.

His voice was soft as he approached. "Vallah, it's okay. It is simple biology. There's no need to be embarrassed. The tension is rolling off of you. I'm sorry I teased you." He cupped her face with his hands and pressed his lips between her brows. It was nice—soothing.

"What was that for?" It was a difficult decision, to stand there and let his hands hold her face, or to step back where she had more control. She held firm and looked him in the eye.

His lips curved into an easy smile. "To let you know you're safe. You're among friends. I know how women were treated on Earth, and that's not going to happen here. You choose who you bed down. No one will ever make you do anything you don't want to. It's also a good time to clue you in...we Asgards have a very high sex drive. This may make you feel aroused more often than you may be used to."

"Oh," was all she could utter. Her breathing was getting labored the longer he held her so close.

"I can feel your apprehension. You want me to kiss you?"

"No. Yes. No, I mean...I have no idea, it's just with you so close..."

He closed the small distance between them. His lips a hair away from hers. "If you're going to object, now is the time." When she said nothing, his lips met hers. When his tongue grazed her bottom lip, she pressed into him, deepening their kiss.

Kissing a mere stranger so passionately wouldn't have been in her thoughts before. But here, with Thor, feeling such a pull toward him, she no longer cared. She was desperate to find out how accurate her dream really was.

He broke the connection, but held her close. "I can feel your thoughts, Vallah. You need to be sure before we continue."

"Feel my thoughts?" The heat of embarrassment sent her face ablaze.

"I can't hear them. Not really. But Asgards are connected. I can feel what you want, and I have no problem telling you I want the same thing. You're the most beautiful creature I've ever laid eyes on. But I don't want to rush you." He stepped back and took a deep breath. "You have been through an awful lot, and this might not be the best idea."

Fact was it had been over a year since she'd had sex. She'd never had sex in her new body, and she could think of worse people to experiment with than the attractive man in front of her. He'd been attentive since her rescue, and she'd noticed.

She'd already decided not to waste her second chance. Now was the time to prove it to herself. Without another word, she turned and walked to the bed in front of the fireplace and knelt down. She looked up to see him still standing where she'd left him, looking at her.

Thor peeled off the shirt he'd just put on and walked to her. He knelt in front of her, scooping her face in his hands once more, devouring her with kiss full of hunger and need. He rolled to his back, taking her with him.

His hands rested on her ass, pulling her into him as they continued kissing. He rolled them over, resting on his elbows above her. His lips trailed from hers, down the nape of her neck as he popped the buttons loose on her shirt. Once it was opened, he took the hard bud of her nipple into his mouth.

An explosion of sensations overwhelmed her, and they'd barely started. She thrust her fingers into his long hair. It was thick and silky, the loose tendrils tickling her stomach, teasing her flesh, as he kissed on her breasts. With one strong tug, he had her shorts past her knees.

Her legs quaked as he began stroking his hand from her hip down her thigh until he pulled one leg open. His lips brushed against the skin, down to her naval. Anticipation and need had her heart thundering in her chest when his tongue finally stroked her lower lips. She fisted the blankets below her and moaned as the warmth of his mouth enveloped her pussy.

Every cell in her felt like it would explode as she became dizzy with pleasure. With expert skill, he brought her to the edge, then retreated, brushing his lips against her inner thigh. Her legs shook; her heartbeat thundered in her ears.

"I can't wait," he gasped as he pushed his pants down and kicked them off. He settled between her legs, resting at the precipice of her entrance. His lips crushed into hers. A small whine of need made its way from her mouth to his when he finally pushed into her slowly.

Whether it was her new body, or the fact that Thor was well endowed and skilled at using his equipment, she didn't know, nor did she care. With every thrust from Thor, she thought she'd lose her mind. Her vision became blurry as he drove into her, and breathing became difficult. She was at the cusp of a very large explosion, and she was holding on to reality as best she could.

In a swift, fluid movement, he withdrew, flipped her on her stomach, and entered her once more. Her dreams didn't hold a candle to the reality that was Thor inside her. His hand snaked under her chest, over her throat, until he was cupping her chin as he drove into her from behind. He held her firm as he increased in his ferocity. The sound of Thor's pleasure in her ear sent a shockwave through her. It was Vallah's undoing. She cried out as her ecstasy reached its peak, and she began riding the largest wave of her existence.

He gave one final thrust before collapsing next to her.

Her body gave out and she crumpled beside him, trying to catch her breath. "Wow." Aftershocks from her orgasm were still rippling through her body.

He gasped and laughed. "I couldn't agree more."

"Okay, I get it." She laughed, giddy from the feel-good endorphins that were coursing through her veins.

Rolling over to face her, he propped his head on his hand. "Get what?"

"Why you are all half naked. It's humid as hell on this planet."

"Thank you, Vallah. It has been a very long time since I've made a connection with a woman. I know it had to take a lot of courage to give in to your desires. I'm honored that you trusted me."

What did a woman say to that? "You're welcome? But seriously...all of these perfectly attractive women around here? You haven't *really* been alone, have you?" The shake of his head gave her the answer. "Why?"

"I had a wife. We were exploring planets to seed and she fell into a cavern. The damage was too much for her body. We couldn't save her." He sat up, resting his arms on his knees. After clearing his throat, he smiled at Vallah. "I have yet to meet anyone that lived up to the perfection of my wife."

Suddenly, she felt as if she'd taken advantage of him.

"Until you showed up, naked, on my ship. It was the first time I'd felt the heart beat in my chest since then."

It was then that reality crashed in on her. "Oh my God...we didn't...we didn't use protection."

"Protection from what?" His eyes were wide, confusion

painted on his face.

"From pregnancy. What else?"

He collapsed on his back. "Oh man, I'm sorry. I didn't think. You don't know how we procreate." He shot back up and grabbed her hand. "We, uh…. we don't ejaculate unless we want to. And you don't drop an egg for fertilization unless you mean to. The flaw in the human design was that my ancestors were looking to grow a population quickly. So they had the female cycle every month, releasing an egg, and the men ejaculate each time. This was fine in the early stage, but as you know, the planet quickly became overpopulated. Well, relatively speaking, of course."

Sweet relief washed over her. "So I guess I have a lot more to learn than I thought, but it's good to know I won't have any surprises."

Thor stood and held out his hand. "Come on, let's go take a dip in the lagoon to rinse off, and then get into the city so you can see your mother."

CHAPTER NINE

When they stepped out of the stargate on the other side, it was dawn. Vallah hadn't considered the time change as the planet orbited its star.

They walked hand in hand until they reached the city's edge. He began pointing out the features of the city, explaining each building. "We won't allow too many cities on the planet because they generally come with pollution, water, and sewage issues. But a few will allow the technology and people to be more centrally located."

"I hate to be needy, Thor, but I could really use a pick-me-up. Is there anywhere to get a coffee or tea?" She was painfully aware that she didn't know how their money system worked, but she was certain she had none to her name.

He put his arm around her shoulder and squeezed. "Of course. I'm not thinking how much has happened since you arrived. Hell, you haven't even slept yet."

"I did sleep for three days straight!" She smiled. The feeling of elation still soaring through her body made her feel lighter than she ever had, even with the new, larger body.

He led her to a small café where they were served

coffee and rolls, for free. Thor explained that they didn't want a bartering system of any kind, to prevent anyone from acquiring any more wealth than another human or Asgard. Everyone would be expected to contribute to society. For some, that meant pouring coffee. For others, it meant practicing as an astrophysicist. It was brilliant. People could do what they loved without the fear of starving to death.

An Asgard man nodded as he passed. "Commander Thor."

"Macario," he replied.

"Commander...tell me how that came to be." Vallah peeled off a piece of roll and stuck it in her mouth. The strong flavor of nutmeg danced on her palate. It was comforting to be able to detect flavors she knew on this foreign ground.

His smile caused his eyes to crease, hiding his deep blue eyes. "My father, he always pushed me to do better, do more."

Vallah chuckled to herself. "What's his name, Odin?"

He did not return her smile. "Yes, we retain the same cycle of family names."

"Seriously?" She knew the old Greek and Norse mythologies. The Amazons had insisted she learn her history.

"Sort of. My father's name is Odin, but he's not *the* Odin. I'm under no obligation to name my daughters Magni or Thrud."

"Thank the gods! Those are horrible names." She smirked and nudged him under the table with her foot.

"My wife said the same...I'm sorry. I didn't mean to bring her up again." His shoulders fell as he gazed into his cup.

"Thor. Thor, look at me." When he did, she smiled. "I've never been married. However, I assume if I did marry and I lost that mate, part of them would stay with me forever. I'm thankful that you feel comfortable enough with me to talk about her." Who was she to get jealous over a dead woman, anyway?

"Your mother should be awake. How about we go check in on her?" It was an obvious change of subject, but she was eager to see her mother.

They walked down the city block to the hospital. He spoke with someone in charge and they were immediately led to her mother's room.

"Vallah!" Valerie stood on shaky legs and held her arms out. Vallah wasted no time stepping in for the embrace.

"We need to get some meat on your bones, Mother." She kissed her cheek.

Valerie waved her off. "Don't you worry about that. The Asgard doctors are already pumping me full of nutrition, and the therapist is helping me get my muscles back. It feels good to be in my true body again." She eased into her chair. "My goddess, look at you. You are stunning, Vallah!"

"Mom, you know Thor?"

She bobbed her head. "By reputation only. The last time I saw him, he was teething."

Vallah squeezed the top of her nose. "Hang on...that math doesn't add up. You say your wife passed twenty years ago, but the last time my mother saw you...you were teething."

Valerie smiled at her daughter. "Time...years are measured when the planet revolves around the sun. My best estimation, this planet takes almost three Earth days to revolve around its star. That's just this planet. Top that with the fact that the Asgard aging process is markedly slower than that of humans...it's easily explained, Vallah. It's just that your education hasn't included much in time and space. The Centurion vaccination will actually make the humans last almost as long here as they did on Earth. Well...around two hundred and twenty years or so here, I assume."

Hearing her mother speak of math and science was

new. Of course, the last time they spoke, Vallah was only eleven.

They spent the next hour catching up. Valerie refused to give much in the way of details regarding her captivity, most likely to spare her daughter, or possibly to avoid reliving the situation herself. Thor had excused himself to run a few errands.

"You've chosen wisely. He is very handsome. His father will approve, I'm certain." Valerie winked at her daughter.

"I'm sure I don't know what you're talking about." They'd never had the first discussion about relationships. She wasn't ready for it yet.

"My sweet daughter, the Asgards can tell. I can tell. We're not human. Once you realize you operate on a different frequency, you'll understand you can't hide anything from one of your own kind. Let's not forget that I'm still your mother and our connection goes a bit deeper." She shook her finger.

The Asgard doctor from the ship, Judith, interrupted their conversation, much to Vallah's relief. She handed Valerie a cube that resembled the cube Thor had given Vallah on the ship.

"I'm so full," Valerie complained. "I really cannot take another right now."

"Ma'am, we need to get your calorie intake up nearly six times what it is now. I can do it intravenously, but it's better to get your stomach working again." She shoved the cube at her again.

Vallah became angry. "She said she doesn't want it. Come back later."

"You do not understand. She's very close to death right now." The doctor shook her head.

An idea struck her. "How much real food do you have here?"

"There's an entire kitchen. Why?"

"Because, those cubes make you feel so full so fast, it's

probably overextending her stomach. Let's get her some real food. It will make her body feel like eating." She stood and looked to her mother. "You still like the foods you enjoyed when I was a child...right?"

Valerie grinned at her daughter. "Of course...you going to prepare some fine Southern cuisine, are you, Vallah?"

"I'm going to see what they have to work with and I'll be back. Don't you dare leave this room! We have so much to get caught up on."

After Valerie agreed, Vallah followed the doctor to the kitchen. They ran into Thor on the way, and his curiosity caused him to follow.

Once in the kitchen, Vallah began looking through the food stores. She found a small vegetable that looked like okra. She peeled it open. The consistency was about the same. She threw some in the large bowl she found.

She continued digging through until she found nearly everything she needed and began cooking. "I can't believe I have to use coconut oil to fry. God help me if this doesn't taste right."

Thor laughed and continued to roll up a batch of peanut butter cookies. "Tell me how sweets will get your mother healthy?"

Vallah rolled her eyes. "The main ingredient there is peanut butter, which is full of protein. Mom is more of a pecan sandies sort of woman, but these will do. Just keep making the little balls like I showed you. I really can't believe I remember these recipes."

"It's your Asgard brain, Vallah. It's thirty percent larger, and memory recall is a huge part of that." Thor placed another ball on the tray.

"Ma'am." An orderly entered the kitchen. "I have no idea what you're cooking up in here, but the humans can smell it and they're going crazy."

"Because you're feeding them those cubes. Humans are really motivated by smell. It's taking them home...to their home that has been destroyed."

The orderly nodded. She tapped a few buttons on a panel. "Your session here has been recorded. With your permission, I'd like our cooks to review the footage and recreate some of your recipes."

"While my mother is here, you should get the recipes she has stuck in her head. That woman was a fantastic cook." Vallah smiled at Thor. "My father used to complain about his pants being too tight quite frequently."

Thor looked to the orderly. "Valerie Sigrid, 6B."

The orderly nodded and then left them alone.

Thor helped Vallah make up a tray of three plates.

"You leave this mess and those leftovers to me." It must have been the cook who spoke. She was the most rotund Asgard Vallah had seen yet. "I have some human patients that smell something called fried okra, and they're threatening me with my life if I don't give them some."

Vallah pushed the tray full of peanut butter cookies toward the cook, who picked one up and took a bite.

"Oh my…these are addictive."

"I've been recorded on that thing on the wall. You should be able to make more of these. The recipe is pretty easy." Vallah patted her on the shoulder. "Find a human that can cook. I swear, we—I mean, *they* are led by their stomachs."

The cook stuffed another peanut butter cookie in her mouth and nodded. "Soon as I get this mess cleaned."

Apparently Thor couldn't wait. He picked up a cookie and took a bite. "Wow. They're so soft."

****

With a happy doctor and a mother that was overly full and napping, Vallah felt comfortable leaving.

"Okay, Thor, spit it out. What's going on with my sister?"

"You're picking up on your Asgard waves already, I

see."

She shook her head. "I cannot explain it, but yes, I have a very strong feeling you know something."

"She's missing. The doctor didn't want to keep her sedated, and she was only alone for a moment. I'm taking you now to see the physician in charge."

He'd already anticipated her needs. It had gone beyond sex...he was looking out for her.

Vallah questioned the physician for a while, but the poor Asgard doctor was confused. "Patients don't just vanish, and none of the cameras detected her leaving her room, much less the building. She was very agitated and angry. I'd ordered a psychological evaluation, but that never happened. I apologize, Vallah, I wish I had better answers. This...this is new for us."

A familiar face looked lost as he made his way down the hall. "William!" Vallah cried.

When he spotted her, it took him a moment. "Vallah, my God, what did they do to you? Where's your ring?"

She started to explain when Thor interrupted.

"Who is this?" As if being nearly two feet taller than William wasn't enough, Thor stood unusually close to William so he'd have to look up to him. It was anything but subtle.

"Thor...this is the man that saved my bacon on Earth."

"Bacon?"

"He saved my ass!" Vallah pushed him gently back a foot from William. "I owe him my life." William was a decent man, and having Thor try to intimidate him made her angry.

Thor's shoulders eased down. "You look lost. Can I help you?"

Seeing his shift in demeanor caused Vallah to relax a bit.

William nodded. "I'm sorry. After waiting for hours, I've been told my sister is here getting treated for some traumatic disorder something or other."

William gave Thor her full name, and Thor spoke with one of the staff. He returned quickly with a hopeful expression on his face. "Wow…William, I'm sorry. It seems that the ordeal with the planet had your sister very upset. It brought out a lot of things that she'd been hiding deep within herself. I'll walk you to her room. It'll most likely settle her to see someone she loves."

William shook his hand. "Thank you! Thank you very much!" As soon as he let go of Thor's hand, he threw his arms around Vallah. "Thank you, too. You…you look different, but good. You look good. I'm really relieved to see you made it too."

Vallah felt anger boiling inside her, but it felt odd, like it didn't belong. "It's really good to see you too, William."

After walking William to Karen's room, Vallah and Thor headed for the stargate.

"Are you okay?" he asked after several minutes of silence.

She shook her head. "I can't explain it. I have nothing but fond feelings for William. But when he hugged me, I felt angry. That's so ignorant. He put his life on the line to save me. Why would I be angry?"

"Because you're finally tapping into that Asgard connection." He looked defeated. His shoulders slumped as his feet shuffled forward.

"Thor?"

He stopped walking. "It was me! I was the one who was angry. You just felt it."

After the day they'd had together, she was exasperated. "Really?"

"I'm sorry, Vallah. We'd just made a connection, and it occurred to me that he was the husband you spoke of, and I…I can't apologize for how I felt."

She wanted to be angry, to make him grovel, but the fact of the matter was he already had the look of shame and embarrassment all over him.

"Thor?" She grabbed his hand. "Thor?" she said again. This time, his eyes met her. "You can feel however you need to feel. But do not try to intimidate my friends. Okay?"

He straightened his shoulders.

"And...I don't know what's going on between us. You've been married. I've never had a serious relationship or even thought it was a possibility. The only thing I do know is that I like it very much when you're near me and that the sex was unbelievable." She looked around her, the stargate building off to the left, the city behind her. "I have a second chance at life, and I'm not willing to waste it. So I'm certainly not going to waste it being mad at you."

He threw his arms around her and squeezed. "Thank you. Thank you again."

"You're welcome." She hugged him back. "Do you want to make it up to me?"

"Anything you want."

She pulled back to look him in the eye. "Is there any way I can stay in your private little hut tonight? I'm not used to communal living, and this has been the longest day in history."

His jaw fell slack, but only for a moment before he gave her one firm nod. "It would be my honor."

CHAPTER TEN

When the sun rose, it peered through the glass, warming Vallah's face and waking her from her slumber. She rolled over to see Thor fast asleep. She was more than disappointed that fatigue and one glass of wine had knocked her out before she could try to get a repeat performance with Thor.

Looking down at the Asgard man lying next to her, she felt something inside her stir. The only relationship experience she had was with Seth, and it had been nothing more than sex, even though he'd professed feelings for her. True, she'd felt something for Seth, but hadn't thought twice when he'd left. Thor, on the other hand, had shown decency and concern. He didn't make her feel dirty for sleeping with him already. He had apparently worked hard to get to his status as commander.

He'd suffered tremendous loss, something which Vallah understood. Would she finally settle down and create a life with a man, the way things used to be? Could she imagine having a family of her own? She knew very little about being Asgard. How would she teach her children their heritage?

"Hi," he said as his eyes fluttered open. "Did you sleep

well?"

"Like the dead." She tried to hide the embarrassment of him waking to see her staring at him by crawling out of bed…as if she had somewhere to go.

"I was thinking," he said as he sat up. "I never did get a chance to show you all of our technology in the city." Before he could say more, though, he pulled a small device from his pants and glanced at it. "Shit!" Leaping from the bed, he ran toward the opposite wall. When he pressed on what looked like a small, round stone, a panel slid open.

An older-looking Asgard woman's face appeared on the screen. "Commander Thor! I've been trying to reach you for hours!"

"Report." He didn't apologize, nor give any explanation.

"We have no less than twenty females who have fallen off the grid. We cannot locate them, and I highly doubt they wandered off without being noticed." She shook her head. "A review of security footage reveals nothing. They disappeared in the same manner as the Sigrid woman."

What has my sister done?

"I will be in the city within the hour." The panel went dark.

"The men are probably trying to reclaim their property." Vallah was certain that the men who'd been gifted wives were not going to stand for them being liberated.

"That is probable. However, we still have the Centurions to deal with. Last I knew, they were not in this sector, but they do have their spies." He pulled his pants on. "We are going to go to the main house and get you a change of clothes. You're coming with me."

She couldn't argue with that. Being in on the action and having information that may lead to her sister was all the motivation she needed. They ran to the main house, Vallah taking the steps two at a time to her room. She found her favorite clothing, her leather pants and shirt, cuffs and boots. Once dressed, she gathered her weapons and met Thor in the main area. He was explaining the situation to the others.

"Baldwin, go to the Amazons at once. They can track better than any of us. I also want a headcount. We need to know exactly how many women are missing, human, Asgard, and Amazon alike. Freya, I want all of the intel we have on the Centurion's influence on our other protected planets." Thor continued to dish out orders to the others.

When they went to leave, a small glass vehicle awaited them. The spherical vehicle floated a foot off the ground. She followed his lead and climbed inside. It soared fast as a plane toward the stargate. Vallah kept her questions to herself and watched as the building opened up, the stargate already activated. They entered the gate in their vehicle and came out the other side. It was nightfall in the city.

The craft zoomed through the city until it came to a halt in front of a glass building. "Stay close. Keep your questions to yourself until the meeting is done, please." He climbed out of the vehicle and Vallah bailed out, practically running to keep up with him. They took a lift to an upper floor, and when the doors opened, a room of thirty or so worried Asgards stood.

"Commander Thor, I've reviewed all of the footage twice," an Asgard man said. "They must be using some sort of transporter similar to ours. The women walk out of camera view and aren't seen again."

Thor nodded. "Any chatter?"

The Asgard man who spoke next had hair black as oil, and eyes that were so dark brown they reminded Vallah of mud. "Nothing, sir. I've questioned everyone in the area, with negative results."

"Humans don't just disappear. These women are our responsibility. I want answers!"

"Start questioning the human men." Vallah didn't hold back. "Look, I know you're suspecting other, uh, races. But I am telling you, they viewed these women as personal property. These were men of wealth and stature I am talking about. They will still have pull among the other humans. And while you may still consider them children, the human race has advanced since the Centurion visit."

"That's very nice, newcomer. But humans don't have beaming technology, and where would they beam to? Some leftover rock that used to be Midgard?" The Asgard man with the black hair spoke with such disdain in his voice, it made Vallah's blood boil.

"And who are you?" she spat.

Thor stepped between them. "Farouk, that's enough. Vallah has a valid point."

Farouk...the same Farouk Thor had mentioned wasn't happy that they were living among the humans.

"I'll question the humans," Farouk said as he narrowed his eyes at Vallah.

Vallah wanted to shove her fighting stick firmly up his ass.

Thor chuckled.

Great, he's using his Asgard feelings or whatever...

The older Asgard woman whose image had appeared in his house finally spoke. "This is a matter of some urgency. I understand the Amazons are already in the forests. We've contacted the Nyx for their assistance as well. For now, we're on high alert and we've doubled security around the females."

"You've separated the men from the women?" Vallah completely disregarded Thor's earlier request to hold her questions.

The older woman nodded. "Until we get the humans settled, we thought it best to keep the women from their captors."

Vallah pinched the area between her eyes. "You've also separated families. No wonder William was so upset." She took a deep breath. "Look, I know this was a huge undertaking and I really do thank you for saving as many as you could. But humans act a lot like pack animals.

Separate the pack, and they sort of lose their minds. They're lost, scared, on a foreign planet, and oh, by the way…their entire way of life has just been ripped to shreds."

"What are you saying?" Thor asked.

"I'm saying that some of these women may have felt safe with their husbands. Some are separated from their siblings, sons, fathers, and grandfathers. They may be sneaking out to see if they can find their families." She looked at Thor. "I'm sorry. I know I was supposed to keep my mouth shut. But I think a good place to start is figure out who is missing and who they belong to. Reassure them that they are only separated for the moment, but that you're getting this thing sorted out." She looked around the room at the look of shock on their faces. "Jesus, I haven't even had coffee yet and I thought of this. You guys didn't?"

"Freya, you're in charge of tracking down their families. Baal, you must organize a meeting place so that these people can reunite if they wish. But make this up to the women, it's their decision. Understood?" Thor continued dishing out orders until the group disbanded.

Vallah felt guilty for disrespecting his wishes and searched for some sort of feeling from him.

"Let's get you some coffee. I want to pick your brain." He grabbed her by the hand and led her from the room, onto the lift to another floor. Several Asgards were sitting enjoying food and drinks, chatting with those around them. Thor went to a panel and looked at Vallah. "What, uh, would you like?"

"I usually have coffee and cream. I'll take whatever I can get." After he spoke into the panel, a large mug of steaming coffee with cream appeared. Vallah wrapped her hands around it like it was a priceless artifact.

*

If Vallah only knew the countless combinations of caffeinated beverages at her disposal, Thor feared he'd never get her away from the synthesizer panels. There she sat in her combat gear, ready for a fight at a moment's notice, and she was stunning.

He watched as she cupped her mug with both hands and sipped at her coffee like it might be the last cup she ever enjoyed. He highly doubted the humans had anything to do with the missing women, but her ideas weren't without merit.

"You were very young when you left Earth." *Of course she was, you idiot. What a way to start a conversation!*

"Eleven."

Vallah had stayed in his home, slept in his bed, curled up next to him as if she'd been doing it her whole life. Asgard women didn't do that. Not unless they were in for the long haul. But there was so much she didn't know. She could take on other husbands, other wives…would he be able to keep her?

"Going with your theory, why do you think the women would want to go back to their captors?" He sipped at his own dark coffee and watched her as she looked at the ceiling while he tried to contemplate her answer.

"My sister."

"I'm sorry? Your sister?"

"When I went to rescue my sister, not only did she not want to leave, she wanted to see me captured. Snow, her, uh, husband, was sleeping in bed with three naked women. She was sitting alone in her room, crying. Yet…she wanted to stay. He gave her something, some sort of security. Maybe it was the wealth. I don't know, but she didn't want to leave. It still doesn't make sense to me, but if she could lose her mind and want to stay with that piece of filth, the others may as well. It's what they know…what's familiar."

"And right now they're scared." He was beginning to see her line of thinking—her beautiful mind that had adapted and accepted her Asgard identity with ease.

"Exactly."

She could be an invaluable resource, but she had so much catching up to do. "Vallah, there is so much you need to learn, but there's much you can teach as well. I'm sorry for asking you not to speak. That was very rude and assuming. I want you to know I value your opinions."

She paused mid-sip and placed her mug gently on the table. "Thank you."

"I'm going to give you a quick history lesson, so bear with me. The Centurions have been our enemies since the time of our seeding of Earth. They didn't like the fact that we were so arrogant. They were right about a lot of things. But, their vaccine was designed to eradicate you, as I told you before. I think their plans are more nefarious now."

Vallah's eyes widened. She was taking in everything he had to say. It made him want to devour her lips once again. His cock twitched at the thought. He had to focus.

"How so?" she asked.

"Earth was the last planet to be made aware of the vastness of the universe, and the fact that…well, other races exist. They've been interfering on other Asgard-protected planets. This is why our transporters strip you of everything but your base DNA. All disease or other foreign bodies are removed, then you're reassembled."

An Asgard woman walked past them and smiled at Vallah. She had the Valkyrie tattoo on her forearm, and it seemed to have drawn Vallah's attention away from the conversation.

"That's the fourth hawk tattoo I've seen in here. Do you mark your women too?" Her brows were drawn in.

"That's the Valkyrie mark. It's a rite of passage for the women of the Asgards who make it to warrior status." He shook his head. "So no, we don't mark our women. It's a coveted mark that all Asgard women strive to attain. If you see one, it means they fought in battle to defend humans, Asgards, or our allies."

Her mouth curved up into a gentle smile. Her eyes

began to dance. "I like that thought. So if I fight in battle, I can earn a mark? That's a lot more desirable than having one forced on you."

He could not imagine the horror of being forced to wear a mark that indicated your fertility, or your marital status. It was no different than an animal marking their territory. He was happy the transporter not only removed her breeding mark, but the marital mark she'd worn. Thor knew he wouldn't have been able to stand to see that. He hadn't felt anything for a female since his wife died. He'd had a few sexual partners, sure. Anything beyond that was just too difficult.

His lifelong friend, Seth, approached off a long mission to one of their protected planets. "Heard we have some problems…You just couldn't keep it together while I was gone, could you?"

Thor grabbed his forearm and pulled him in for an embrace.

"Seth! It's good to see you return safely. Let me introduce you."

When Seth turned to face Vallah, her face fell blank.

"My Bella?"

"What did you say?" Thor looked between the two of them.

The color drained from Vallah's face. "You're one of them?"

His heart hammered in his chest. How did these two know each other? "What's going on?"

"You look fantastic as an Asgard woman! I knew you would! Stand up, give me a hug." Seth stood with his arms open.

Vallah stayed in her chair for a moment, looking up at him as if he were covered in manure.

"Bella, it's me," Seth said with his arms still open.

Thor searched for what she was feeling. The only thing he felt was confusion, but wasn't it his own?

Slowly, she rose and hugged him.

His heart felt as if it rested on his boots.

"I'm glad to see you doing well." She reclaimed her seat, eyes still wide, with no expression on her face. Thor still couldn't detect any feelings other than his own confusion, and it was doing little to quash his heartache.

"I see you've met my best friend in the galaxy." Seth smiled, picked up Vallah's coffee, and took a sip.

Never in the fifty years of his life had Thor wanted to smack his best friend. At this very moment, he wanted to put his nuts in a molecularizer and send them into space.

Seth looked at him. "Don't you want to know how I am? About my mission? What is going on with you?"

Thor had to start thinking again. "We have a situation." He filled Seth in on the missing women, one of them being Vallah's little sister. It was a welcomed distraction from the confusion he felt and the look of shock on Vallah's face that only served to twist him more.

"Humans can't do this. They're not advanced enough. Well, not the earthlings, anyway." Seth shook his head. "I'd bet my whole fleet it's the Centurions. Say, I'm starving. Have you two eaten already?"

"Not advanced?" Vallah looked at Seth, and for the first time, Thor picked up a hint of anger. Anger he could deal with. Seth calling her Bella just irritated him.

Seth looked at her and laughed. "Hardly."

"Thor," Vallah said as she turned to him, "I'd like to go now."

His ass was out of his seat so fast, he nearly took the table with him. "Yes, we have much to do. Seth, we'll catch up later."

*

Outside, Vallah was finally able to breathe. Seeing Seth had caused her insides to stir, and not in a way she had expected. He'd been an Asgard this whole time...but how had he changed his appearance?

Either way, you don't profess your love to someone you've lied to over and over. That's not love, that's subterfuge.

She decided it didn't matter. They hadn't seen each other in over a year, and she'd just slept with Thor, and wasn't about to go around sampling every Asgard male in a fifty-mile radius.

They'd walked for a good five minutes while Vallah fumed. Finally, she realized that they were in a part of the city she didn't recognize. "Where are we going?"

Thor shrugged. "You looked like you were on a mission. I'm following you."

"What?" She stopped, turned to look at him, and burst out laughing when she saw the look of concern on his face. "You were just going to keep walking wherever I went without saying a word?"

He held up his hands. "Look, you're an Asgard woman, and if life has taught me anything, it's not to piss of a woman who is obviously hot under the collar. Top that with the fact that you were trained by the Amazons..." He shook his head. "No way I'm tempting the safety of my balls by questioning you."

"So you're not going to ask me what's wrong?"

"Nope. I will only say that I'm here *if* and only *if* you want to talk about it. We can walk around all night if you wish." This giant commander looked like a cat about to flee.

She shook her head. "I should probably tell you. Is there somewhere we can sit?"

"How about a drink?" He motioned toward a building on the corner.

"Sounds good."

They entered a bar. Several Asgards sat with human women, guarding them as they drank.

"I thought the humans were on lockdown," she said.

He shrugged. "They're all wearing monitors and security has doubled. No harm in letting them socialize. The men are a few miles away and have a bar of their own."

She looked at the wary women, drowning their sorrows in whatever they were drinking. "Yeah, a few stiff drinks might do them some good."

After finding a somewhat secluded table, Thor ordered drinks for them.

"So...Seth," she said with a sigh.

"Vallah, you don't have to talk about it if you don't want to. I can see whatever it is has you troubled."

She looked up from her drink. His light brown hair made his blue eyes sparkle. Even with the concerned look on his face, he was stunning. The relationship was brand new, and considering how she felt about Seth's dishonesty, she felt she should come clean with Thor.

"I, uh...well, Seth used to come to the village to see me." She wanted to throw up. Surely Thor wouldn't take this well.

"See you?"

She picked up her drink and took a big swallow. Whatever he'd ordered her went down like fire. "Jesus! Is this what you drink?"

"It's what I drink. I have no idea what you drink." His leg began to bounce.

Vallah waved over a waitress. "Do you have anything less harsh than this?" she said as she swirled her drink around.

"What did you drink on Earth?" The red-haired woman with the pointy ears stood patiently as she waited for Vallah to answer.

"Can I bartend?" A human woman stood, wringing her hands. "I just...it's what I did back home. I have to do something besides sit around or I will lose my mind."

The waitress looked to Thor, then at the bartender. "I don't see why not."

The woman came up and held her hand out to Vallah. "You must be the woman who thought she was human. I've heard a lot about you. Do you know what you like to drink?"

People are talking about me? "I have no idea. I used to drink mead, but it was nasty. It was just the only thing that was around other than wine, which tasted like juice to me. Can you make me something in the middle?" What an awkward turn of conversation. People were discussing *her.* As if she were *someone.* But she wasn't. She was just a child when she left, and a woman trying to save her sister and survive in the meantime when she came back.

When Vallah was left alone once again with Thor, she took a deep breath. "I'm just going to spit it out. We were introduced so I could explore my sexuality."

He had no reaction.

Vallah held her breath as long as she could. "Say something!"

His brows furrowed in as he shook his head. "Is that it?"

"Thor…we had sex…a lot."

"Okay? Why does this have you…ohhhh." He slid his hand across the table and put it on hers. "Human chastity. Listen, Vallah, we're all sexual creatures. Of course you had to explore with someone. I realize that you may think it's bad, but I assure you, it's not. Many of us have multiple partners. Some settle for just one in the end, others settle for more. Just…were you in love with him?"

"What? No. I mean, he said he loved me, but I don't think I shared the same feelings." She put her head in her hands. "I can't believe I'm having this discussion. Wait… settle for more? What do you mean, more?"

"We don't live by the same restrictions, Vallah. Some of us marry more than one person. This is why I wanted you at the main house, and we've barely spent any time there. I wanted you to see for yourself, to talk to the other women. But truly, it's okay. So long as you—never mind."

The human woman set a large glass in front of her. "Alabama Slammer, and trust me, you can slam it. It's very smooth."

She thanked the woman and began taking large sips of the drink, which was actually quite tasty. Multiple partners…it seemed like such a foreign thought. "What about homosexuality?"

"Homo what?" he asked.

"You know, two people of the same sex?" She laughed at the ridiculousness of the language barrier when it came to slang and clichés.

"What about it?" Confusion twisted his face again. She'd really like to see him laugh for a change.

"Do the Asgards do that? Or was it banished like on Earth?"

"We love who we love. There are no rules, though honesty is paramount in an Asgard relationship. I'm assuming humans aren't that different."

"You'd assume wrong." She finished the rest of her drink in one gulp. "Let's go before this hits and I get tipsy."

CHAPTER ELEVEN

Back on the Asgard side of the planet, Thor insisted on spending time at the main house. Vallah was a little unsteady on her feet from drinking on an empty stomach. After a big lunch, she and Thor went for a dip in the lagoon. Marika joined them, as well as a few others whose names Vallah could not remember. It wasn't easy for her to strip naked in front of strangers, but they'd all done it. Bathing suits were not among the Asgards' list of clothing.

The tepid water was relaxing her. She allowed her eyes and her mind to wander to the surroundings. The new planet certainly had its charm, with lush tropical foliage and wildlife. She saw a toucan soar from one tree to the other and smiled. The bird looked so free, so happy to live in its new environment. She could be too.

"Beautiful, isn't it?" Marika floated up next to her. "I really love our new home world."

Vallah couldn't agree more. "I can't believe I've lived here for a decade and missed all of this."

"All of this happened pretty recently. You didn't miss much. The first few years of your stay with the Amazons, there was a protective bubble around the village to maintain the balance of oxygen. We did a decent job getting these plants to maturity, but it was a challenge."

"Do you have any idea how unsettling it is that everyone seems to know more about me than I know about myself?" She fought the pout she felt already on her face.

"Have you any idea how difficult it is to see a little girl you want to play with but you're forbidden in case you accidentally tell the truth?" She smirked. "I wanted to be friends. Thor's father forbade it. So I hid in the forest and watched you. I pretended to be there next to you, learning how to fight, or reading a book, discussing the history within."

Vallah laughed. "How long did you stalk me?"

"Three of your Earth years. Then I reached maturity and had to leave."

"Well, Marika, we can be friends now. I don't really know anyone beyond the Amazons, and I haven't seen them since I arrived." She grinned at the almost albino Asgard woman. "Why don't you tell me about yourself?"

A soft smile spread across her alabaster skin. "My mother died in the first battle against the Centurions. That's why I was sent to stay with the Amazons until either my father returned or I reached maturity. When my father returned, I studied communications and culture while this planet was coming out of its infancy."

"Are you married?"

She sank down in to the water. "No, I am courting a few with potential, but nothing serious yet."

Thor's words replayed in her mind—multiple partners. "Can I ask you a personal question?"

She bounced in the water, her breasts floating dangerously close to Vallah's arm. "Of course you can. I know there's a lot about our culture that you will want to learn, and my personal answers to your personal questions may help."

Vallah considered her for a moment. "Can you tell me about *your* ideal marital situation?"

Marika floated on her back and stared at the blue sky. Vallah was taken aback by her lack of apprehension that her nude body hovered on the top of the water for all to see.

"I'd like two husbands and a wife, ideally." The idea of a foursome made Vallah's brows rise toward her hairline. She wanted to ask more questions but felt apprehensive. What if she offended Marika?

Marika righted herself. "I take it by your silence that stuns you?"

She shook her head. "Stun is not the right word. I have more questions, I just...I just don't want to be offensive."

"Just ask. I'm really open, and I know you're trying to figure things out, Vallah. It's okay."

With her reassuring words, Vallah took a leap of faith. "Why that specific combination?"

"I'm an only child. The thought of having a woman I'm close to, well...that's very nice, indeed. The two men can be companions, leaning on each other in times of need in a brotherly sort of way. If one or two is killed in battle or lost in some other way, then the children still have a male and female role model."

"So...would her children be your children too?"

"Of course," Marika smiled. "I had two mothers. They were wonderful. I only have one father left, but the one who passed was really great with me when my first mother died. He let me cry on his shoulder for days."

Vallah chewed her lip as she considered her question. "So...do you have sex with them all?"

"Why wouldn't I?" She shook her head. "Intimacy adds another layer to our connection." She pointed across the lagoon to a woman relaxing in the water between two men. "That is Toka, and her two husbands, Daniel and Salamon. Daniel and Salamon do not have a sexual relationship with each other; however, she has a relationship with them both. That trio over there? The two men do have a sexual relationship and she has one with them both as well."

"Geeze, how do you know about their private lives?"

Marika smiled at Vallah and tilted her head to the side. "Unlike humans, we're very open with our sexuality. We aren't bashful to share the details. We have sex frequently and talk about it openly. For instance, I've slept with your Thor many times."

"What?" Her heart sank. Was nothing sacred with these people?

"Calm yourself, Vallah. Thor was lonely, as was I. Of course, we weren't right for each other. We just kept each other company in times of need. It's been a few years since we've spent intimate time together. I let him know I wanted to try to find mates of my own to settle down. He was very sweet and made a few suggestions. There's not one thing for you to be worried about." She placed her hand on Vallah's forearm. "I know you've been raised with human perspectives on love and relationships. But I challenge you to open your mind."

Vallah sank below the water, allowing it to envelop her. When she came back to the top, she wiped her eyes and took a deep breath. "I don't even know where to start. There is a strong feeling inside that I should embrace my new life and be grateful for this second chance. But honestly…where do I start when it's all so foreign?"

"Well, I would start by asking Thor who he'd like to join you in bed." She giggled. "You really must try two males at once. Your body will feel like it's going to explode with pleasure."

I'd better get out of this lagoon before she has me in a full-blown orgy. "I'll think about it. Thank you for talking with me."

"How are things over here?" Thor swam up behind her.

Oh God, don't ask.

"We were just talking about Asgard relationships. I suggested Vallah chat with you about trying to bring another male in—see if she likes it."

"Of course!" Thor put his arm around her. "Would you

like to choose someone, or would you like me to make some suggestions?"

"I feel like I've fallen and hit my head." How could they be so free and open? Was it just one big gangbang all of the time?

Thor and Marika exchanged confused glances. "Your head hurts?" Marika asked.

She squeezed her eyes shut. "No. My head is fine. I just...maybe I wasn't ready to talk to Thor about that just yet. You just brought it up and I hadn't considered it."

He put his finger under her chin and made their eyes meet. "It might be nice for you to see that Asgard men worship their women rather than enslave them. But we can discuss this when you wish."

"For what it's worth, Vallah, I feel the connection between you two. I believe the fates have brought you two together, and you shouldn't ignore that." After a sigh, she continued. "I'm actually quite jealous of the energy between you."

Energy?

As if Thor could read her thoughts, he answered, "Remember that we operate on a frequency? You will get in tune with that frequency once you become accustomed to your new body. But Marika can feel the connection between us. Granted, it's new, but I feel a very strong pull from you that I just can't help but answer."

You do?

"Can anyone join this discussion?"

Seth's voice set Vallah immediately on edge.

"I'm leaving," she announced as she began wading toward the water's edge.

"I'll go," Vallah heard Marika whisper.

"Vallah! Wait!" Marika's feet splashed as she made her way to the water's edge. Vallah grabbed a towel and began drying off.

"I'm sorry. I just, I can't, not with Seth. I'm still angry."

"Oh, I felt that. I just don't want you to be alone." She

grabbed a towel and wrapped it around her waist. "Let's go inside."

Marika started a pot of water while they changed. Back in the main area, dressed and feeling less vulnerable, Vallah took a seat. Marika slid a cup to her. "Tea. It's actually my favorite tea. Calms my nerves."

"I could use it. There's so much on my mind right now."

"Just talk, Vallah. I'm a good listener. Maybe I can help you."

Vallah looked up at her. Her blonde hair was still damp and slung over her shoulder. Her blue eyes like ice managed to look warm.

"I'm concerned because the human women are coming up missing. I think the men are reclaiming them, and that worries me. My mother is doing better but still needs time to recover. My sister is among the missing but may have something to do with it all. I just…I just started with Thor when Seth showed up and ruined everything. I don't know the first thing about being an Asgard, or using any frequency. I feel so out of place I want to scream. And that makes me angry, because I really want to embrace who I am." She held up her mug. "So this tea needs to be pretty magical."

"Breathe, Vallah. Seriously, take a deep breath. Hold it for a moment. Then let it out."

Vallah did as she suggested.

"The frequency, I can teach you. Communications is my specialty. Seth…well, you're allowed to be angry. It'll subside. The humans, we will find, I can assure you. Your sister? We'll find her. I'm sure she's frightened and hiding like the others."

Vallah opened her mouth to object.

"But if she's not, and they're not hiding, we'll find them all. I promise, the Asgards have taken this very seriously. The communicators went crazy when it happened, and many of us are working on the problem. As a matter of fact, my vacation has ended quite abruptly. Tomorrow I go into the city and back to work."

"Wow." She'd answered all of her concerns in nearly one breath. "So, you can teach me how to find this frequency stuff?"

She stood from the table. "Grab your tea, we need a quiet place."

Vallah followed her through the maze in the giant tree until she opened the door to what must have been her own private bedroom. "This will work. The main area has too much traffic. I want you to sit on the floor."

Vallah squatted on the floor, took a sip of the tea, and placed her mug on the floor. "Okay, now what?"

"I'm going to feel things as strongly as I can and walk you through it. Are you ready?" After a nod, Marika closed her eyes.

She concentrated on what she was feeling. As if a flute on crescendo, a feeling of glee came in slowly, then it faded. "I think I felt it. Was it happiness?"

"Yes! See, you've got it already. You just have to trust your instincts." She knelt next to her. "Let's try again."

Once again she concentrated. It felt as if someone had her hands on her shoulders and pushed her away. "I don't like that. What were you thinking?"

She smirked. "That I hated you. Which I don't. I had to work for that one."

"So you said you feel a pull with Thor. What does that feel like?"

With a quick shake of her head, she apologized. "Sorry, I can't make you feel that, but I can describe it. Say...say you had a rope around your waist. And suddenly, it had tension, then pull. That's what it feels like when you're near two people who have pull on each other. When he's near, you want him closer. When he's close, well...you want to mate." She grinned. "It's so romantic. I really do envy you. Now, I did you a favor, it's your turn to do one for me."

"Anything."

She took Vallah's hand. "If you do consider taking an Asgard wife into the mix, will you promise to contemplate me as a possible wife?" She bit her lip. "I know it's a new idea and I know it's odd considering…however, I feel a connection. I have since we were children."

"Marika, you're a fine woman. I just…I don't…I've never even thought about women that way."

She waved it off. "That's no matter. It's a new idea. All I'm saying is that in the time I've courted others, I have never felt the way I feel around you. I used to watch you and think about how strong you were, on the inside. You were thrown into a situation, but you put your head down and worked harder than anyone in history to achieve what the Amazons wanted you to achieve and more. You didn't cry. You didn't fail. You worked…hard. That's so admirable. I admire you so much. And I said I would like the intimacy, but if it's too much for you, then I would consider vacating that desire to be close to an Asgard warrior as strong as you."

Vallah no longer had to try to feel frequency. It was coming off Marika in waves—excitement, adoration, and…something she couldn't identify.

If she was going to keep an open mind, then she didn't want to tell Marika she wasn't interested. She would honestly consider the proposal. "All I can promise is that you would be my first choice."

She grabbed Vallah by the cheeks and kissed her forehead. "Thank you! Oh, thank you."

"Oh my God!" Vallah gasped.

"What?"

"Seth has felt my anger but…he has acted so clueless. I wonder why."

"Stupidity. He thinks if he acts as if nothing is wrong, you'll forget why you're furious." She rolled her eyes. "Men."

****

Vallah sat on the bed, alone, pondering her new life. She hadn't any idea how she was supposed to fit in, or adapt, but she was determined to find her place. Her entire young adult life was spent learning combat skills. Perhaps she could join the Asgards as a warrior. After all, they were her kind, and they protected humans. What objection could she have?

There was the possibility that their politics and morals wouldn't match her own. She had spent enough of her life in solitude. It was time to be part of something bigger.

The sounds of the house grew in volume. She went down to the main area to investigate.

"Commander, they've invaded Eros. The humans are in distress. The Centurions are poisoning them." A younger man was pleading with him. "We must fight back! Thousands are gone. Thousands!"

Many Asgards had tears in their eyes. Vallah fought the urge to jump in and ask questions. She held her tongue and observed, moved by the sniffles in the room. They truly felt the loss of human life. Then the sorrow hit her...the Asgards' emotions in that room were strong. They truly loved the humans, not like pets, but...as children?

"We need to organize, Bensi. We can't just load up in our ships and fire at the planet."

"I know, Commander, but we must act quickly before more innocent humans fall victim to the Centurion agenda," Bensi pleaded.

Vallah finally saw Thor, the weight of the decisions he had to make wearing on his features. His shoulders were raised, and suddenly, Vallah felt something hit her in the chest. Anger and rage filled her every cell until she tasted the metallic tinge of blood in her mouth.

"They have pushed us far enough. The Centurions will feel the full force of our wrath for harming our children.

Let us never forget that the humans existed because we were lazy and entitled. It was our arrogance that brought them into existence. We are accountable for their futures. I will seek counsel from Odin and reach out to the Nyx and Orithia. Organize our fleet." He made a grunting sound and pounded his chest.

When the room began to clear, Seth and Thor spoke quietly in the corner. This was not the time for anger, so Vallah pushed it out of her mind and approached. "Excuse me."

They turned and gave her their attention.

"I'd very much like to help." She cleared her throat. "I believe I can be of some assistance."

"Unlikely," Seth said dismissively and turned back to Thor, whose eyes were still fixed on her.

"Go on."

"Is there a stargate ring thing on that planet?"

Seth rolled his eyes. "Just stargate."

Thor stepped in closer. "Yes. Why do you ask?"

"It seems to me the reason you never seem to defeat the Centurions is because you load up in your ships. Well, if they have the same level of technology you do, then they can see you coming. They'd never expect you to come charging through the gate."

"We've never considered using the gate as a means of defense. Only a few people can go through at a time."

Vallah grabbed a container from the counter. There was something coarse in it, like salt. She poured it on the table and drew a circle. "But you can go in two or three at a time and defend the others as they step through until you have a decent-sized army. Since they're not expecting you, and you've never attacked that way, it's unlikely that the gate is heavily guarded." She drew little figures on the outside of the gate. "If you have a plan that the person on the left guards the left and the person on the right aims right, and the next group that steps through does the same as you advance, you should be able to get fifty to a hundred through before they have time to react. At most, they probably have a few guarding it so the humans can't use it to escape."

Seth and Thor exchanged looks across the table. "That's a sound plan. Still, I need to consult Odin about contacting our allies."

"No, you don't. You are commander of this fleet. Your father retired a long time ago." Seth put his hand on Thor's shoulder. "I know you respect him. So do I."

"It's not up for discussion. I will consult him. We haven't called on our allies in generations." He looked to Vallah. "I would like you to accompany me and explain your plan to him."

Meet his father? No. No, thank you. "I'm sure you can recite it to him."

He furrowed his brow. "We leave in a few minutes."

Is that an order? "Fine."

Seth stood looking dumbfounded. "You're taking her?"

"Don't sulk. You're going too. Get your things in order." With that, Thor headed out the door.

*

Thor stood in awe watching Vallah draw lines in the sweetener, displaying line of sight as they would invade through the stargate. It was riveting to watch her explain in detail, confident in her plan of attack. He could not deny her savvy combat skills.

No one had used the stargate in such a manner. Attacks were always by starship, which caused massive loss in resources for each battle, both in the stars and on the ground. Warriors were blind when beamed aboard the surface, giving the enemy the advantage.

Vallah's plan would reduce casualties for them and their allies. Odin would be impressed.

Even more impressive was her ability to set aside her anger for Seth to outline her idea, even with Seth being so dismissive. If his wife could see her from the halls of Valhalla, surely she'd approve. Hell, she might have even suggested her as a wife when she was still alive.

The sadness was leaving Thor bit by bit. Vallah felt like a warm blanket to a child, a breath of fresh air after being underwater...she felt like home. It had been so fast and so natural for him. Still, it was all new to her. She might not stay with him. She might forgive Seth and pick up where they left off.

He had to stop obsessing. It was time to see his father, and Odin would pick up on the connection. He knew Odin would give his blessing. Even still, a bit of anxiety plagued him.

With great haste, he readied the ship to take them to Gefn and sent a message ahead so his father could be ready to receive them. He'd need Odin's assistance to organize the allies. Thor might have been Supreme Commander, and have the respect of the Asgards and the Amazons, but it was his father who held the respect of their allies.

Respect that was deserved and earned. It would be his one day. Until then, he had no issues asking Odin for his help.

What troubled him most was Vallah's suspicion that her sister was more than likely the cause of the disappearances rather than assuming her innocence. While they had tracked Vallah on the planet, things had been too chaotic for anyone to know what had happened between her and Faith in that house. The only thing he did know was that Faith had been unconscious when they'd located the two of them and beamed them aboard.

Vallah had seemed genuinely embarrassed when Marika mentioned expanding her sexual experiences. He'd never understand that element to human nature, and while she might have reclaimed her Asgard body, inside her head, she was still very much human.

And his sweet Vallah was just starting to receive the

Asgard frequency. What would she do when she figured out that Marika was already head over heels for her? He wouldn't mind having two wives. He'd enjoyed sex with Marika before quite a few times until she'd decided she was ready for a more permanent situation. Thor just hadn't been ready to open his heart yet.

Until Vallah appeared on his ship.

CHAPTER TWELVE

Vallah stood at her closet. *What does one wear to meet the father of the guy you just screwed?* Dressing for comfort, she put on her Amazon combat gear and went to the main area to wait. She was about to meet Thor's father. The man who helped Valerie conceive her. She still didn't know who her father was. She'd have to get an answer to that question soon, and Odin would know that answer.

Seth came down the stairs dressed in black slacks and a black shirt that hugged his body in all the right places. She forced herself to look away. She'd not drool over the man that had lied to her.

"Still holding that grudge firmly in place, I see."

"Fuck off, Seth. I have nothing to say to you." She crossed her arms over her chest to keep her hands from wringing his neck on their own.

Something in his pocket beeped. "That's for us, unless, of course, I'm supposed to fuck off on my own."

Gritting her teeth, she followed him outside. A small spacecraft was hovering just above the ground. It was triangular in shape with a small bubble in the center. The outside looked dark, grey, and metallic. A door opened on the side and a small ramp extended to the ground. She followed Seth up the ramp.

It was the second time Vallah had boarded a spacecraft, this time of her own volition. It was much less jarring to walk aboard.

"Strap in," Thor commanded.

She sat in a seat and pulled a harness down. It locked in place on its own.

"Once we leave the atmosphere, you can walk around. But you don't want to be knocked down by the inertia." Once they were both strapped in, he angled the craft toward the sky and pushed the steering mechanism forward. The force made it hard to breathe. Her back was pushed firmly against her seat until the sky turned from blue to black. The stars shone bright, and the force that was pushing her back had subsided. The harness released and lifted.

Thor pressed a few symbols on the glass panel in front of him and then got up from his seat.

"My father is very traditional. When we meet him, we briefly take a knee and lower our heads. It's a sign of respect for his age and wisdom." Thor took a deep breath. "Seth, I expect you to show him the level of respect he has earned."

Seth's face turned red, but he kept his mouth shut.

"Vallah," Thor said before he took another calming breath. "Whatever you need to say to Seth, say it. We can't walk in there with this tension. He, I mean my father, will feel it and it will cloud the discussion."

"I've said all I have to say." She looked at her feet.

"Those two words didn't really speak volumes, Vallah," Seth objected.

Thor chuckled. "Two words?"

Anger began boiling to the surface. She didn't deserve to be in the hot seat. "Yeah, I told him to fuck off." She turned to face Seth. "But if two words weren't enough for you, how about this? Fuck *the hell* off, you lying son of a bitch! You knew. You knew the whole time that I wasn't human. Hell, you even took drastic measures to look human just to make the lie worse. I couldn't hate you more than I do now, and I don't see that changing for all eternity!"

"Well then. I think that clears things up a bit." Thor smacked Seth on the shoulder. "Good luck, buddy. I'm going to meditate."

Meditate?

Thor disappeared to the rear of the ship. Seth finally stood up and began to pace. "You are under the impression that I wanted to lie to you, Vallah. That it was fun for me to know what was coming and not to be able to say a word."

"Oh? What was wrong? Someone cut your lying tongue out of your head?" She crossed her arms over her chest again, partially holding her insides in place since they felt as if they would explode.

"Thor's daddy gave strict orders to have your fate play out as it should. Meaning that had I told you the truth, I could have been punished, even jailed. It would have been treason to interfere in the life of an Asgard sleeper."

"Oh, that's a crock of shit, Seth. We were alone…a lot. You didn't mind fucking me, but to risk telling me the truth was just too much to ask."

"We kill people for treason, Vallah. Disobeying the commander can mean a death sentence. Is that what you wanted? You wanted me to tell you the truth that you would learn a year later and risk my neck for that? I put my life on the line for people nearly every day. Excuse me for not putting another Asgard at risk just so you didn't have to wait to learn the truth." He huffed. "You're entirely more selfish than I ever imagined. To think I professed my love for an ungrateful, self-centered narcissist."

Ouch! Okay, so expecting him to risk his life to expose the Asgards to her was a bit much to ask, but how was she to know?

"You never even bothered to apologize." She averted

her eyes, looking out the windshield at the planets they were passing. It still dazzled her that people really flew around in outer space.

Seth plopped back in his seat. "I am sorry, Vallah. I wanted to tell you—that day, before I left, I nearly showed you my true self. I wanted to. But Odin said you wouldn't approach life the same. That if they managed to save Earth from annihilation, that you'd never feel like you belonged. He said it was in your best interest, and I had to trust him. Hell, he wasn't happy that I was seeing you in the first place."

Tears stung her eyes. Every part of her life had been dictated and controlled. Was that making her angrier than Seth's lie by omission? Was he just an easy target? She hadn't been controlled since making it to the new planet. Thor was letting her take the reins.

Before she could find the words to make peace with Seth, the craft began a rapid deceleration and pointed toward a dying planet. It was grey and desolate-looking...at least, that was how it appeared until the craft closed the distance. The planet wasn't a planet at all, but a giant fabrication...made of what appeared to be metal.

A female voice echoed within the ship. "Greetings, Commander Thor. Gefn is prepared to receive you."

"You have control, Command," Thor said as he walked back to the bridge.

"Gefn?" Vallah whispered to Seth.

"It's the name of the starship. It's sort of a makeshift home world where our elders hold up." He smiled. "Loosely translated, it means 'protective goddess.' Fitting, don't you think?"

Very fitting.

The craft slowly lowered toward Gefn. Large doors opened while the craft was lowered inside. Then the doors closed above them as the area lit up all over at once. A loud tone sounded three times before a higher-pitched tone sounded.

"That means the airlock is secured. We can get out now," Thor explained.

He pushed a button on the wall and the doors opened and the ramp expanded downward. She followed the two men down the ramp, where they were met by a very old-looking Asgard woman and two armed guards. "Warmest greetings, Commander Thor. Your father is very pleased you made the journey. This way."

Vallah's eyes couldn't take in the view fast enough. Several other small ships were in the area. Some older-looking than others, which was weird because it was technology far more advanced than anything she'd seen before.

They entered a white corridor, lights turning on prior to them entering the next area. They approached a set of metal doors that slid to the side, opening what looked like an elevator. Once inside, Vallah tried to see how the thing was operated, but it appeared to move on its own.

"Curious one, your guest," the old woman said.

"This is her first time on Gefn, or anyplace like it," Seth answered quietly, "Valkyrie."

Valkyrie. Vallah had heard that word before. This older woman was a hallowed warrior among the Asgards. Suddenly, she felt a tremendous amount of respect for the woman escorting them.

The silver-haired woman turned to Vallah and smiled. "It is controlled by my mind, dear."

Vallah's face turned red. How had this woman known her exact thoughts? "Thank you."

When the doors opened again, everyone stepped off the elevator except their escort. Vallah's heart throbbed in her chest. She had no reason to be nervous, yet she felt a bit of anxiety. The room was white and stark-looking. There were no decorations whatsoever, only two long couches and two chairs that faced the couch, with a small, oval glass table dividing them. She followed Thor to the couch and took a seat next to him, with Seth on her other side.

When the man rounded the wall and came into view, Vallah was astonished. Thor couldn't have looked more like his father unless they were twins. The only difference separating them was white hair and wrinkles. She was so absorbed by her astonishment, she hadn't noticed Thor and Seth taking a knee and bowing.

"Vallah!" Seth whispered.

"Oh!" she gasped. "Oh, I'm so sorry, sir. I…"

"Nonsense, Vallah, I wouldn't expect you to be familiar with Asgard custom. My, my, do let me get a good look at you." He extended his arms, placing his palms on her biceps. "Your mother's daughter, for certain. You make a fine Asgard. It's very nice to make your acquaintance."

"Thank you. It's an honor to meet you."

Odin took a seat in one of the chairs facing the three of them. "It's customary for us to share a beverage." As if on cue, a human woman entered the room carrying a tray. It was a shock to Vallah to see her there. "Thank you, Wanda."

"Do you require anything else?" Her black dress reminded Vallah of a maid's uniform on Earth. Her dark hair was wound in a French twist.

"No, thank you. I appreciate your service." Odin nodded to her. It appeared to be respectful, but Vallah could only assume.

"What brings you to Gefn, my son?" Odin asked as he poured a warm liquid from a small white pot into very small white cups. He handed one to each of them. When they all began to drink, Vallah brought the cup to her lips and tasted, trying not to choke on the hot alcohol that was burning her mouth. She forced herself to swallow and fought hard to contain the cough that was brewing in her throat.

"The Centurions have invaded Eros, Father. Thousands of human lives have been lost, and we fear for the safety of those that remain. This is the fifteenth planet they've affected that we know of. Rumors of their poisonous vaccine on other planets are beginning to surface. I believe it's time we seek the assistance of our allies and shut them down indefinitely."

"Thor, to wage an assault of that magnitude is not without catastrophic collateral damage." Odin tossed back the remainder of his drink and placed his cup on the table. "We cannot ask our allies to sacrifice their assets in such a manner, and we don't want to exacerbate the loss of human life."

"Agreed. Vallah has a plan that would give us a significant tactical advantage without utilizing much in the way of material assets." Thor turned to glance at Vallah, who sat speechless. "Also, I believe it to be a plan that would lead to far fewer casualties."

Odin's mouth curved into an easy smile. "I'm eager to hear your plan, dear. I have no doubt the Amazon training has served you well."

She nodded. "I suggested we use the stargate."

Odin's brows shot upward in shock but soon settled. "There are risks to utilizing the gate. If your plan fails, the enemy may begin to shut down the gates on other worlds to prevent their use. It could prevent the evacuation of other worlds."

She placed her cup on the table and folded her hands in her lap. "I wouldn't suggest using it unless you could mount a full-scale attack. I don't know how Asgard morality works, but humans take killing very seriously."

Odin shook his head and furrowed his brow. "As do we. I'm still concerned with the loss of life. However, doing nothing is not an option. We've taken as many diplomatic approaches with the Centurions as possible. They continue to violate our treaties and poison our humans. They must be stopped." He looked to Thor. "I assume you need my help contacting our allies?"

"Reassurance from the old guard along with the new might calm any concerns. The Nyx have been less than helpful with our cause."

Odin stood from his chair. "Follow me."

They followed him to the other side of the room and through a door that led to what looked like a conference room. "Vallah, your sister is missing. Correct?"

"Yes, sir. How did you know?"

He brought a photo up on screen. "Is this her?" It was a still photo of her sister shaking hands with a Centurion. The large forehead ridge was a dead giveaway.

"Yes, unfortunately." Her shoulders fell. "How could she?"

Odin brought up another photo. This time, there were dead bodies lying on the forest floor. Holes were blown in their chests. The people appeared small, their skin was lavender in hue, and their hair looked like it hadn't seen a comb in decades.

"I doubt the Nyx will have any objections. This is what the Centurions did to the Nyx who were visiting our colony on Abjura." He shook his head. "They're increasing in violence and have become downright barbaric." He sighed. "The Nyx are such a peaceful race, they didn't see this coming."

Vallah stepped closer to the display screen. There were ridges on the bridge of the nose of the victims. Other than that and their lavender skin, they looked very human. She thought it odd how familiar all of these aliens looked to her.

"Is this one a child?" She pointed at what looked like a teenager lying in the pile of bodies.

Odin sighed. "Probably equivalent to a thirteen- or fourteen-year-old human." He closed his eyes briefly, then looked up. "You three, stand shoulder to shoulder."

Without question, Thor and Seth closed ranks next to Vallah. Thor opened a long wooden box and pulled out a staff...a traditional Amazon warrior staff. The Amazons that had trained her had only had one, and it was an ancient relic, according to them. The rosewood had been polished to a shine, a large garnet embedded at the top.

He looked them over. "Men, stand at attention. Vallah, as you are."

Thor and Seth folded their hands behind their backs and pulled their shoulders tight. Content with their appearance, Odin pushed a few buttons and a Nyx man appeared on their screen. "Elder Odin, warmest greetings."

"Warmest greetings, Elmhoard. I'm here with Commander Thor, his second-in-command, Seth, and the Valkyrie-in-waiting, Vallah."

Valkyrie-in-waiting? She fought to keep her face straight and hide the surprise of Odin's phrase.

"Warmest greetings," Elmhoard said with a nod. "I assume you're contacting me about the Centurion violence."

Odin put his fist over his heart. "I'd like to extend my deepest condolences for your losses on Abjura. Your suspicions are correct. We're reaching out to you as the leader of the Nyx. My next contact will be to Queen Ayala of Orithia. It is time we join together and stop these atrocities. The Centurions cannot be allowed to slaughter and poison our people."

Elmhoard looked down and took a deep breath. "Odin, I have always warned against your fondness for the human race. Their self-destructive behavior is beyond my comprehension." He paused and looked back toward the screen. "However, some of them on older planets are able to evolve beyond the self-destructive instincts they have. Some are showing signs of telekinesis and telepathic abilities. More and more of them are showing promising signs indeed."

Vallah noticed that the Nyx man's expression never changed. She couldn't tell whether he was sad, angry, or just…indifferent.

"Beyond the need to study the humans further, the Nyx are prepared to join forces with the Asgards, providing that you can persuade the Amazons and the Orithians to join. It's time for us to unite as one to stand against the Centurions. They've become a parasitic race. If we do nothing, they will consume every planet they touch. That cannot be allowed to happen. If they refuse to coexist, they must come to an end."

"I am humbled by your wisdom. If the Amazons and the Orithians agree, will you send a delegation to the new Midgard?"

Elmhoard smiled. "Elder Odin, you would not have contacted me if you didn't think the other allies would agree. The delegation will depart before the next solar rotation." The screen went black.

Odin turned and smiled. "Well done. Vallah, now I need you to stand next to me. The Orithian queen responds well to our Valkyries. This time, I wish for you to speak. Explain your plan to her in as much detail as you can."

"Yes, sir." *But I'm not a Valkyrie.*

Odin turned to his son. "Thor, the Amazons are ready?"

"Itching for the fight, sir."

"Excuse me," Seth finally spoke. "Vallah, the Orithians can seem...condescending and rude. It's part of their personality. They like to see if they can get you riled up. That sharp tongue you use against me would serve you well with them. It'll earn their respect. Just...don't appear upset, even if you're raging inside."

Odin and Thor both agreed.

Thor grinned at Vallah, as if he didn't have any concern about her wit. "Yes, it's a test of control. Use your wit. Everyone ready?"

Once again, Odin pressed a few buttons and the screen illuminated. It took everything Vallah had not to let her jaw fall open. These women shaved the sides of their heads and had a thick, braided mohawks. They were covered in tribal tattoos and had bigger muscles than any of the Amazons. Their men rivaled their appearance with long, thick mohawks, tattoos, and very little in the way of clothing. But what really floored her was the couple fucking in the background.

"Elder Odin, I had no idea you liked to watch." The woman was sweating and completely naked.

"Warmest greetings, Xanra. I need to speak with Queen Ayala. It is a matter of great urgency."

A woman crawled off the man she had mounted and sauntered to the screen. "Odin, to what do I owe the pleasure?"

Odin cleared his throat. "Our allies are joining forces to put a stop to the Centurion threat. We're reaching out to you to send a delegation to Midgard Two."

They really need to give that planet a better name.

Her green eyes danced in the screen. "Thor, you really had to run to daddy for help?"

In response, Thor lifted his chin. "It is only the very young that do not respect the wisdom of their elders, Queen Ayala."

Vallah wanted to reach through the screen and slap the woman in the mouth.

She stroked the breast of the woman standing to her left. "And why would we get involved?"

"Vallah," Odin said as he stepped aside.

"Because they've begun killing our allies, kidnapping our women, and poisoning our people. I don't wish to have a Centurion slug as a master, and from the looks of your men, I highly doubt you'd find any pleasure from a Centurion cock."

The woman's mouth fell open.

Slam dunk.

"And I suppose you have a plan, Valkyrie?" She was no longer distracted by the nakedness around her, and focused on Vallah as she laid out the plan to use the stargate.

"This will only work once"—she lifted her chin—

"before they begin destroying every stargate they find. With the assistance of your warriors, we can crush them like the bugs they are." *Did that sound conceited enough?*

The queen's attitude shifted and she began dishing orders to those around her. "I will have every warrior at my disposal landing in your Midgard city within two solar rotations. Be ready to receive us."

"We are indebted," Odin said with a bow.

"You can settle that debt by lending me a few Asgards. Thor and your Valkyrie would do nicely." She winked into the screen before it went black.

Vallah finally released the breath she was holding.

Seth scooped her up and hugged her. "That was completely amazing. Wow, Vallah. Just...wow."

Was he forgiven? For now, she'd let it go. She didn't have the time or energy to be angry.

"You're a fine Asgard. I couldn't be more proud unless I was your father." Odin nodded. "You made the right decision bringing her, Thor. As I suspected, you are an exemplary leader. Now, if you two will excuse me, I need to show something to Vallah." With his hand in the small of her back, he began to lead her away. She looked over her shoulder at Thor and Seth, both of whom had bewildered looks on their faces.

Why was he leading her away? Where was he taking her that his own son couldn't join them?

"I'm sure you have many questions." Odin put his hand on a square panel and part of the wall slid to the side.

"Some."

"I feel your anxiety, my child. You can relax. Nothing bad is going to happen." He smiled at her as they walked. "But it's high time you got all of the answers you seek. The first of which is your paternal ancestry."

He slid open a drawer, which had some sort of control panel in it. "His name is Vidar. Using human relations, he would be my father's cousin." An image of an Asgard man was displayed on the panel. His hair was dark, and Vallah's eyes matched his more closely than her mother's. She had his nose.

"He passed away a long time before Valerie used his genetic material to conceive you. You must understand that it was a great honor for her and very difficult to keep you hidden, safe, and unaware of the truth. There's no need to keep anything from you any longer."

She looked from the display into Odin's eyes. "I could have handled the truth."

"And if you had known the truth, then what? Would you have taken your training any more seriously? Would you have tried to save your sister? Would you be as empathetic toward the humans? Doubtful. The plan was for you to grow up human, with human experiences. We have made many mistakes with the human race, but the one thing we did right was to preprogram empathy in their neural nets. Some ignore it for their own gain, of course. I don't regret my decisions. Not one bit. I understand your confusion and anger. I can only imagine how you felt the moment you realized you were...different."

"I highly doubt that. Everything I knew about myself was a lie." She hated how bitter she sounded.

Odin didn't seem to mind. Instead, he smiled at her. "Really? Everything? Other than your appearance and your size, what is different?"

She considered his question and had nothing to reply. Really nothing was different other than her looks, size, and ability to receive the feelings of others.

"Now, we need you to be an Asgard. I have a piece of technology here from the Ancients. If you put your face in the device, it will bring you up to speed...as if you were born and raised as an Asgard. Our culture, our beliefs, all of our knowledge will be put into your beautiful brain. No longer will you struggle to adapt. It will come naturally."

She was no computer, of this much she was certain. What was this business about downloading stuff into her head?

"I'm not...no, I don't..." she stammered. "That's not possible."

He laughed. "Oh, it's quite possible, it's just very top secret. Upon my death, this knowledge will be passed on to Thor. But until then, even he cannot know it exists."

The room suddenly seemed smaller, and she felt lightheaded. "I have to sit down."

Showing her vulnerability went against everything Vallah stood for, but she thought she'd better sit down before she fell down.

Odin grabbed her by the arm and wrapped his other arm around her waist. "Whoa, girl. You need to stop holding your breath."

He was right. She was so apprehensive about everything she continually held her breath, waiting for another shoe to drop.

He helped her kneel on the floor. "Take a deep breath in and let it out."

She did as he instructed, then did it again. Within seconds, she felt better. "I'm sorry. I don't know what that was about."

He helped her to her feet. "Keep breathing. Now," he continued as if nothing had happened, "you will still retain all of your memories, but you'll have the full knowledge of the Asgards. All you have to do is put your head here," he said as he pointed to the device.

"You expect me to lie to Thor as you had Seth lie to me? I think not." She took a step backward. "Part of that empathy that you cherish is feeling like you are doing something wrong by withholding information from someone. That's the same as a lie. I have too much respect for Thor to lie to him."

"I am aware that you are in love with my son. However, as commander, he is a valuable asset. Should he be kidnapped and tortured for information, what do you think our enemies would do if they learned of an Asgard device that could give them all of our knowledge within seconds?" He closed the distance between them. "Are you prepared to put this entire facility at risk? Thor? Because that's what your inability to keep your mouth shut would do. You want full disclosure? Thor will have the truth, one day. Why is it your decision to choose when he gets this knowledge? When he takes that risk?"

Vallah put her hand on his chest and pushed him back. "Look, Odin, you might be the big man to everyone else, but to me you're just another man. So don't try to intimidate me. You don't think Thor would be tortured anyway? You don't think your son is strong enough to keep the secrets of his people? How little you think of the commander of the Asgard fleet."

Odin looked as if someone had just slapped him in the face. He took a step back and hung his head. "I wasn't trying to intimidate you. I offer my deepest apologies."

"Accepted. Now, it seems we are at an impasse. So now what?" She felt guilty seeing the look of defeat on this elder's face. But she still felt the same.

"If you decide to receive the knowledge, I will let you make the decision on whether or not to tell Thor. But I do ask that you don't disclose the device to any other living being, even under threat of torture." He lifted his chin. It was odd seeing Thor's face so aged and looking so damned stubborn.

Vallah considered his proposal. She already knew what it meant to be human. If she could receive the knowledge as he suggested, she wouldn't go through the aches and pains of tripping over herself to learn what it was to really be Asgard.

"What will happen?"

"You will become unconscious for a period of time. When you wake, you'll have all of the knowledge you need to truly be an Asgard, or rather, to know what that means. It isn't instantaneous, but it will come naturally." He grabbed her hand. "I believe you will one day be my family. I swear on my life that I will make sure you are taken care of. I will catch you when you fall and carry you to the ship myself."

"Will it hurt?" She felt impish asking, but had to know.

He shook his head. "You won't feel a thing."

"Let's do it."

CHAPTER THIRTEEN

She opened her eyes and looked around. She was alone on Thor's bed in his little hideaway. She sat up and took inventory. The last thing she remembered was being in Odin's private office area and putting her face up to a machine. Then, she was waking up at Thor's home.

Was it a trick? She certainly didn't feel or think any differently. Suddenly, she had a craving for coffee and whiskey cake. "What the hell is whiskey cake?"

No one else was around, and she wasn't about to dig through his kitchen, so she headed toward the main house. She stopped in her tracks when she reached the steps. A warm feeling enveloped her—like coming home. It was the same feeling she had when she'd get off the bus and run up to the steps of her childhood home, to her mother's warm embrace.

She closed her eyes and tilted her head up, feeling emotional. After a brief moment, she opened her eyes and headed up the stairs to the enormous house in the tree. Marika was descending the stairway when their eyes met. Suddenly, Vallah felt nothing but adoration and...love?

"You're awake! Thor said you had some sort of spell in his father's dwelling. How are you feeling?" She put her hands on Vallah's cheeks.

"This is going to sound nuts, but I want caife and whiskey cake in the worst way." She'd used the word caife instead of coffee. *That's weird.*

"Okay, there's nothing nuts about asking for the traditional Asgard breakfast, except for the fact that you've only been Asgard for a few days." She ducked and looked in Vallah's eyes, which were averted toward the floor. There were so many things coming at her all at once. It was as if the house in the tree were humming. "Are you sure you're okay?"

"Yeah, just…the coffee, please?"

Marika served her and sat watching her as she ate.

"Dear Goddess, this is to die for!" She stuffed another chunk of cake in her mouth.

"Dear Goddess? Are you sure you're the same Vallah?"

That was it. She wasn't the same Vallah. Something was different. Suddenly, she saw Marika in a whole new light. A young Asgard woman, serving her people, pining for that connection. She was strong yet soft, inviting. She made Vallah feel warm inside.

"I haven't thanked you yet."

Marika laughed. "Thanked me for what?"

"You've been a wonderful friend. I know that you wanted to be friends long ago, but you've made me feel so welcomed…so wanted. Thank you for that."

Her crystal-blue eyes became damp. "Oh, wow. You're putting off a very loving vibe right now, Vallah. You have no idea how badly I needed that."

"I have a weird favor to ask." She couldn't believe the words, or that the idea even came to her mind.

"Of course," she said, sniffing.

"I'm wanting to find my place…my family. I know I shouldn't rush into it. At least, I think I shouldn't. But I don't want to wait, either. If I do, say…try two men…would you—man, this is so awkward."

"You want me to be there for support?" She smiled

and tears spilled down her face. "I can feel what you need. Man, it's really coming off you strong today. I don't know what changed, but it's like you were born Asgard, except it's very strong."

She pushed her plate to the side and focused on Marika. "Listen, I'm still not sure about a wife or any of that."

Marika waved her hand in the air and wiped her eyes. "Never mind. You'll figure that out. But to answer your question, I will be happy to be there to support you as you experiment your relationships."

The smell of roasting meat wafted through the room. "What is that heavenly smell?"

"A feast before the battle. You may have just woken, but it's time for our second meal of the day. The Amazons are feasting with us tonight. The Nyx and Orithia will be here tomorrow evening. We'll have something a bit more formal with them as we prepare to go into battle together."

This was going to happen. She was going to fight the enemy, save her humans, and bond with their allies. *Her humans?* It made sense now. The Asgards viewed humans like children...like *their* children, feeling full responsibility for their safety and well-being.

"Go on, go get cleaned up and we'll walk to the hall together."

Andromeda leaped through the window and sauntered up to Vallah. "You're a sphynx. Why didn't I see that before?" The cat licked her face and nuzzled her on the chin. "It's nice to see you too. I get it now." She scrubbed behind the feline's ear. "You are the great protector."

Seemingly satisfied with her attention, the large cat curled up against the wall and closed her eyes. Vallah shook her head then went to clean up.

****

As Vallah and Marika approached the hall, the smell of

meat grew stronger. Laughter echoed out of the hall. When they entered, several of them were drinking and cheering. Katana was in an arm wrestling match with an Asgard woman.

Tatiana was in the lap of an Asgard man while they kissed one another.

Seth approached with his hands in the air. "Don't hit me!"

Vallah had had enough. She grabbed the back of his head and pulled him in, kissing him hard on the lips. When she released him, his hands had slacked a bit.

"Surrender is exactly what you should do," she teased.

"Does that mean I am forgiven?"

She knew. Somehow she knew the impossible situation he was in and how bad it had to have tortured him. "Forgiven. Don't ever lie to me again, or I'll castrate you."

"What do I have to do to get a kiss like that?" Thor whispered in her ear.

Goosebumps formed on her flesh and she shivered. Something about him had attracted her from the start. The sex had been incredible. The fact that he wanted a kiss after she'd just laid one on Seth made her love him more.

Wait? Love? Is this love? She pondered how she felt for a moment. It was so obvious that Marika and Odin knew it, so it had to be.

"Oh no, Commander, all you have to do is show up." She pressed her lips on his, using his long hair to pull him closer. Her heart swelled in her chest when his arms wrapped around her waist. She could feel his lust vibrating off of him. *This Asgard frequency isn't so bad.*

Deciding it was best she didn't tear his clothes off right then and there, she stepped back and smiled.

"You're feeling better; I take it?" His face was flushed.

"Much. Let's eat."

They spent the next hour feasting and drinking the Asgard equivalent of whiskey. Spirits were high. Many of them were clearly feeling quite amorous on the precipice of battle.

Thor stood and made a toast. "I want to thank our Amazon allies for being the best and closest friends to the Asgards. We've cherished you for many centuries and hope that together, through victory, we seal our bond for all eternity!"

The room erupted into cheer.

"Tonight, we make love, because after tomorrow, the Centurions won't know what hit them!" Thor raised his glass again and many hoots and yells echoed throughout the hall.

Night had fallen, and the hall began to clear out as lovers made their way to somewhere more private. Vallah was left at a table with Thor, Seth, and Marika, who'd already suggested the four return to Thor's private home.

Vallah took one last swig of whiskey. Two men at once was a first for her, and if she were honest with herself, she was a bit nervous having asked Marika to join for support. Alas, plans were already in motion, and the foursome walked to Thor's.

The men walked ahead. Marika lagged with Vallah, and whispered as they walked. "Asgard men are really intuitive lovers. I'll sit off in the corner, and if you feel scared at any time, just look at me. Okay?" She put her head on Vallah's shoulder. "But you have nothing to worry about. I've made love with them both and they're wonderful men."

"You know; human women aren't so open about all that." She laughed. "Before, it would have made me feel…jealous? But now, I feel nothing. It's okay."

Marika didn't reply, and Vallah began to worry she'd upset her.

Inside Thor's home, Vallah's heart began to thunder in her chest. Thor came up from behind her and kissed her neck. "It's all natural. Just do what comes naturally, and if you don't like something, just say so."

His hands slid down the front of her, unbuttoning her vest as he went…his lips and tongue caressing her neck and shoulder as he worked. Seth was already on his knees in front of her, unfastening her belt. She'd been with them both individually, but together was a new story.

She glanced at Marika, who sat in the corner with her hands folded. She offered a gentle smile.

When Seth pulled her pants to her ankles, she stepped out of them, completely exposed. Thor slid her shirt off her shoulders. A chill came over her and suddenly, the fireplace erupted into flame. Vallah jumped.

"That's right, my Asgard woman. You lit that fire." Thor's breathy laugh tickled her ear.

Seth's tongue ran up her slit. Vallah gasped and leaned back on Thor to steady herself. She stretched her arm behind her and pushed it inside Thor's pants, grabbing his rock-hard cock. He was already ready to take her.

Seth had explored her body numerous times, and his mouth on her clit already had her soaring. Her knees became weak with each flick of his tongue. "I need to…the bed."

In unison, Seth scooped up her legs as Thor cradled her shoulders and they settled on the bed. What looked like no more than a fur rug was plush and soft. The tiny hairs tickled Vallah's bottom as they settled in, Seth between her legs, his tongue working magic as Thor slid off his pants. His magnificent cock hovered over her, his knees on each side of her head.

He knelt down kissing her, sucking on her bottom lip. His kisses trailed down her chest until he sucked her taught nipple in his mouth. She cooed and bucked against Seth's mouth. The explosion of sensations overwhelmed her body. While he swirled his tongue over her other nipple, she reached above her, wrapping her hand around his cock, and stroked the length of his shaft. The anticipation of feeling him inside her again filled her with need.

She could barely breathe now, with Seth increasing the pressure, teasing her clit, sucking her in. She pushed against him one last time. An explosion of color washed behind her eyelids as she cried out.

"Good girl," Seth chuckled as he slid her down toward him. He rested his cock at her entrance. "Now show Thor how badly you want him inside you."

Vallah opened her mouth, taking him in as far as she could, sucking and stroking him with her tongue. He let out a growl and planted his hands on the floor to steady himself. "Whoa."

Overwhelmed by a feeling of confidence that she could only assume was Marika pushing it at her, she took Thor into the back of her throat.

Asgard men can go all night. How did I not know this? As the knowledge flooded in, she grew more excited, if that were possible. Endless pleasure. A man who could climax and continue. Why would anyone leave the bedroom? How did the Asgards get anything accomplished?

Seth finally pushed into her, only thrusting slowly for a few strokes before he returned to the robust lover she remembered. She moaned as he pushed into her, and the sensations sent Thor over the edge. She could feel his cock throb in her mouth as he gasped and shook.

He settled on the floor next to her and resumed loving on her breasts while Seth fucked her hard. When he retreated, Vallah looked up to see what he was doing.

"His turn," he said with a grin.

She flipped over and straddled Thor, easing onto his still hard as a rock cock. Her eyes closed as she concentrated on feeling every inch of him. He must have been enjoying her tits, because he resumed sucking on them, the sensation sending lightning strikes of pleasure throughout her body. Seth was behind her, gently stroking her ass.

When his thumb brushed her rear entrance, she froze. "I waited until you were out of that human body for this."

Was it going to hurt?

His thumb was slick with her wetness when he slowly

pushed it in. There wasn't any discomfort, like she expected, so she resumed riding Thor, but slower, as she began to enjoy the ass play from Seth. Still, she was a bit nervous, as it was clear he intended on fucking her there.

She looked to Marika for guidance. Her friend smiled. "It's quite nice."

With a bit of reassurance, she focused on the sensations and pleasure. Thor's mouth was going from right breast to left, his cock pumping into her from below. Seth's thumb was probing her ass, sending waves of pleasure that made her excitement flow.

Finally, Seth wound his hand in her hair and settled his cock at her rear entrance.

"What's with the hair?" she gasped out.

"You're going to go crazy, and I don't want you biting my friend." He laughed for a moment, then slowly pushed into her.

She expected a bit of pain, but to her ultimate surprise, the sensation of being full inside blew her mind. She did want to bite Thor, but it was because her passion was uncontrollable. She sucked on her own lip as her men fucked her.

As if on cue, Marika knelt next to her and stuck her finger in Vallah's mouth. She sucked, hard. "That's good. Oh, it feels so good. I know it does."

Vallah held on to Thor's strong chest and fought between trying to breathe and sucking on her friend's fingers. She felt so needy, so full. The pressure in her began to build again.

"This ass is spectacular." Seth smacked her ass, hard. Vallah squealed and jumped.

Thor lost control as his orgasm grabbed hold of him once again. He jerked, squeezing her tits hard as he pushed into her one final time. With Thor and Vallah mid-orgasm, Seth followed suit. He fell forward, catching himself, palms on the floor. He pulled out of her and fell back on his heel, allowing Vallah to collapse next to Thor.

Marika brushed Vallah's hair from her face. "Spectacular. Right?"

All she could do was nod as she was still fighting to replenish the oxygen levels in her body. She was thirsty and exhausted. It was the first threesome of her life and it had taken everything out of her.

After collecting herself, Vallah grabbed a jug and a stack of glasses from Thor's kitchen. She had no idea what it was, but she was thirsty. She poured them all a serving before she took a sip, realizing it was wine. Thor's favorite wine.

"I'm sorry," she apologized.

He leaned against the wall and crossed his legs. "You could pour this on the floor and still have no reason to apologize. That was beautiful."

"Yes it was." Marika once again appeared emotional. It sparked an idea in Vallah's mind.

"Marika has asked me to consider her as an Asgard wife." Taking a page from Marika's book, Vallah held nothing back. "I think, if she wants me to consider this fully, she should definitely take you two for a ride. I mean, how can she be a spouse if my men don't enjoy her company?"

That was what the woman needed to hear. Vallah could feel her immediate arousal, but a bit of apprehension.

She held her finger up in the air. "I know what you're thinking. I said *humans* would be jealous. I'm not human. I am Asgard. This is how we roll!"

"Roll?" Seth said with a laugh. "We're rolling around now?"

"Just go with it. Dick." Vallah laughed before taking another sip of wine.

Thor rubbed her leg. "What about you?"

She smirked. "Oh, I'm here for moral support and finger-sucking."

There were giggles.

"Except, I want to undress her," Vallah announced.

Thor smiled at her. His beautiful eyes glistened. "Why is that?"

"Because...I don't know about a relationship with a woman. I've never done that. But unwrapping this gift would be an honor...and a good place to start."

Marika stood and walked over to her. "That would make me very happy."

Vallah handed her glass to Thor and stood. "I'm going to give you a gentle peck on the lips. Okay?"

Marika nodded, her eyes wide as she gazed into Vallah's eyes. "You do whatever you want."

Vallah leaned in slowly, pausing before their lips connected. Marika's lips were softer than Thor's or Seth's. She tasted of strawberries and wine. If she were honest with herself, she actually liked it.

She pulled Marika's shirt over her head. Her breasts bounced free, her nipples pretty and pink as they stood at attention. Vallah looked into her eyes and she only nodded. Vallah brushed her tongue over the pink flesh that hardened under her warm tongue.

She cupped Marika's firm breast with her other hand. It was nice, soft and pillowy. As Thor had done, Vallah kissed her way to the next location. She tugged at the waistline of her skirt and pulled it to the floor. She had no idea how to pleasure a woman and wasn't ready to dive in just yet.

"I'm going to let the experts take over for now," she professed with a wink. She took a seat and watched as her men ravaged Marika, who was a much more vocal lover than Vallah. She commanded and led the situation without hesitation.

Vallah envied that freedom and hoped one day she could do the same.

Her friend reached orgasm three times. Each time, Marika looked to Vallah, and it made her heart race. The woman definitely wanted a connection, and a deep one.

Marika had curled up with Seth, who had covered them

both with a thin blanket. Thor patted the makeshift bed next to him. Vallah gladly claimed the spot, backing up to him. He tossed a blanket over the two of them.

He kissed her shoulder and nuzzled in her neck. "You okay?"

"Pretty wonderful, actually." She remembered his words about his late wife only wanting him. "What about you?"

"I'm in love with a woman, but too much of a little boy to tell her." He snickered and put his forehead on her shoulder.

"I think I'm in love with you too. I can't be certain, of course, because it's a first for me." She laced her fingers in his. "But what I feel is pretty fantastic."

"Are you ever going to tell me what happened in my father's office?"

She remembered Odin's words. Thor could be tortured, and then the responsibility of the Asgard knowledge falling into enemy hands would be his fault…and hers. "Maybe, one day. For now, suffice it to say, your father helped me find my inner Asgard."

"Vallah, one day, and I mean *one* day, I would like you to be my wife. Whatever that looks like to you is okay with me. Marika is a fine woman. Seth has been my friend since we were crawling on the floor. But if it's just you and me, I'm okay with that, too." He sighed. "I know it's soon. I know this has been a lot. But I just would like for you to know how I feel."

"It sounds nice, Thor." Fact of the matter was it actually did sound nice. A husband and a family, a best friend as a mate, too. What wasn't to like about that situation?

He began massaging her thigh. The sensation was heavenly. He picked up her arm and slung it over his head so he could have access to her breast. "You have the most beautiful tits. I can't get enough." She felt him growing hard behind her as he sucked on her nipple. "I have to have you one more time tonight."

She opened her legs, granting his cock access again. This time, his fingers worked furiously on her clit as he thrust into her. She was worried about waking Seth and Marika until she heard moans of pleasure coming from them as well.

He filled her completely, every cell in her body ignited where he touched her. "This is Valhalla," he whispered into her ear as he picked up his rhythm. She turned her head, grabbed the back of his head, and pulled him in for a kiss. He'd just called making love to her heaven.

The sounds of Marika and Seth reaching climax excited Vallah in a way she'd never been excited before. She wanted to reach out and touch them both. Instead, she watched them fuck as Thor made love to her. "Beautiful, aren't they?" he whispered in her ear.

They were. Watching them was not only beautiful, but exciting. She began trying to match Thor's thrusts by pushing her ass into him, helping him go deeper. It was erotic, lying on their side, watching as Seth had Marika riding him, her voluptuous breasts bouncing. It felt as if the taboo were gone, yet clung on just enough to heat the room. Vallah buried her face in the blanket as she cried out her orgasm.

She had curled up with Thor, Marika with Seth. When the four were sated and content, they finally fell into slumber.

CHAPTER FOURTEEN

After rising early, they made their way to the city. Vallah went to check on her mother while the other three prepared to receive the allies.

"Vallah!" Valerie stood from her chair. Her muscle tone seemed to be returning.

She embraced her mother. "How are you feeling?"

"Old," she teased. "I'm so very happy to see you."

"Have you heard about Faith?"

She nodded. "That child was never happy. No matter what we did, she was always sneaking around getting into trouble. William and I worked hard to find her a suitable arrangement. I knew Snow liked to have many women, so I figured she'd be left alone more. But honestly, there was no good answer. She's very bitter." After a deep breath, she shook her head. "Honestly, I can't say that I blame her. It was an impossible situation for such a young woman."

She studied her mother, searching for a feeling. "I don't mean to upset you, but I do want to run something by you."

Valerie nodded. "You think she's involved in these disappearances? I thought the same thing. It's quite possible. She'll do anything to feel like she has some sort of power."

"The other Asgards thinks it's all the Centurions. But I have a feeling that there are some humans involved as well." She leaned in toward her mother. "They don't know what the men on Earth were like. I can't seem to make them understand."

"Yet you have the ear, and the eye, of the supreme commander." As Valerie smiled, her daughter blushed.

"It's going to take some getting used to, having everyone know your business." She rubbed her face. "Still, Thor doesn't suspect the men as I do."

She patted Vallah's knee. "Facts, my child. The Asgards need evidence to give any credence to your claim."

"It's not that they don't give me any validation. Quite the opposite. They are questioning some of the humans. It's just that they seemed completely astonished that the men would still think they had any claim to the women, or the ability to take them."

Valerie poured a glass of water and sipped as she thought. "I was a young woman myself when I agreed to return to Earth as a sleeper. It came to be that it was not me who was called to duty, but my daughter. I know the Asgard ways, but...times and things change. You will have to trust your instincts. Do all you can to right the Asgards' wrong. That's our duty, our charge, to repair the damage of our ancestors. This means all human life is your responsibility. Even that of your sister."

"You look like you're ready to leave the hospital. Where will you go?"

"Odin has invited to me to stay at Gefn until I am ready to rejoin the others. I have lost a lot of time, and there is much I have to learn about our recent history. I trust you, Vallah. I trust that you will find these women and your sister and return them to safety."

With a nod, she kissed her mother's cheek. Thor had given her directions to the building where they would be meeting their allies. Though her body told her it was morning, the night breeze kissed her cheeks as she exited the hospital. She only had five blocks to walk and plenty of time to get where she was going. Spotting a café, she hoped to catch a fresh cup of coffee.

"Vallah?" William sat by himself, clutching a hot beverage.

"It's so good to see you! Is this seat free?"

William's eyes were dark and sunken in. He didn't look well. Vallah could feel his anxiety rolling off in waves.

"Please." He stood slightly as she took a seat.

"You look awful. What's going on?" A waitress came and took their order, and as soon as she left, Vallah turned back to William.

"Karen. I can't find her."

Oh God!

"They let us visit every day by the fountain. It's where women can venture out to meet men they wish to see until they feel the women are safe to move about on their own. There are a lot of those giants around—er, sorry. The tall people…security…whatever, they're there to make the women feel safe. Yesterday, Karen didn't show. No one will answer my questions. Others are upset as well. These Asgards are about to have anarchy on their hands." His shoulders slumped. "I fought so hard to keep her safe on Earth. Here, I just…"

She grabbed his hand. "The Asgards are taking this very seriously. As you can imagine, this was a huge undertaking. They are looking for those that are missing. They may be hiding from other humans somewhere on this planet, somewhere they feel safe." She doubted it very much, but it was still a possibility.

"The underworld is starting all over again. People are bartering with whatever they can. But I have nothing. Nothing at all." He looked as if he would start sobbing.

She squeezed his hand for reassurance. "If you had something, you could get in with the criminal element; find out what's going on. Right?" Her brain was working overtime.

"Of course. What do you have in mind?" His lips finally curved up slightly.

"Vallah? What is going on?" Thor stood behind her, arms crossed, and...was that jealousy she felt?

"Thor, I'm so glad you're here. Please sit. I just had a brilliant idea."

He remained standing, his arms crossed, brows furrowed.

"Oh, stop it with the jealous nonsense and sit!"

"I may just be Thor to you, but I am the supreme commander of the Asgard fleet!" He flexed his arms.

"Oh, for fuck's sake, sit down already, supreme dummy! I have a plan."

His shoulders fell, as did his mouth. Apparently, he wasn't used to being dismissed in such a manner. Like a good little commander, he pulled out a chair and took a seat.

"The humans are doing what they know how to do. They're trying to barter. As I suspected, there is far too much anxiety with the segregation of the sexes. I think we should give William some currency. With him leading the underground, we'll have some control and all of the information we need."

Thor leaned in on his elbows and flexed his jaw. "Hold on a hot second. First, we don't have money here. Second, there's no underground on this planet."

"That's what you think," William huffed. "They're trading whatever they can. It's just the human way."

"Wait! Wait! It's coming to me!" Vallah closed her eyes as memories began flooding in. Memories that weren't exactly hers. "You had...phones. You didn't call them phones. They were handheld devices used to make video contact."

"They're called ironsides now...very obsolete." He shook his head.

"Well they're called phones now. Can we get some?" The excitement was overwhelming her.

Thor's shoulders bounced as he chuckled. "Okay, you're too excited. What are you thinking?"

"Let's give William access. He can use them to gain trust with the bad guys."

"Bad guys?" Thor began laughing harder now.

"Make fun of me all you want, but yes, humans with nefarious plans. Bad. Guys. Now, can we get some of these, and he can sneak them to the men and women of his choosing? Maybe in exchange, he can find out something about the missing women. Someone somewhere must have seen or heard something." She wasn't about to let him dismiss her. William's sister was missing, and this would at least give him purpose and maybe even lead to her being found.

"You're too insistent for me not to take this seriously." Thor looked to William. "You can make your old connections?"

He nodded. "In a matter of hours. I just need something to work with, and some way to contact you."

A Valkyrie passed their table, her tattoo catching Vallah's eye. *I can't believe I actually want that mark.* After years of tattoos being forced on her, she'd never dreamed she'd crave one. Now, she wanted to earn the hallowed hawk.

"Meet us behind this building in an hour." Thor looked at Vallah. "We need to go."

The waitress finally placed her cup on the table. Vallah looked at the cup, then up to Thor.

"I cannot deny you, woman! Drink up." He looked at Vallah's hand, which still held William's.

"Commander, Sir, Vallah and I went through something on Earth. I consider her a cherished friend, nothing more. My heart belongs to a woman who is in that building over there." He pointed at the housing for the women.

Vallah retracted her hand and used it to slug Thor in the shoulder. "Yeah, you big dummy."

He rubbed his shoulder and smiled. "Okay, okay. I get it. It has been many years since I felt jealousy. I apologize." He looked to Vallah's cup.

She took the hint and quickly drank her coffee, then followed him out of the café. "I can't believe you are jealous. You literally just shared me with others but you're jealous of William?"

With a heavy sigh he nodded. "Maybe it's just the fear that humans still feel more normal for you and I'm worried that this is still so foreign. Either way, you can skin me later. We need to pick up the pace to get everything accomplished in the next hour." He put his arm around her and hurried her along.

They went to a storage facility where they retrieved the video phones and new power cells. With two boxes full, they hurried to the location where the Asgards were preparing to meet their allies.

"Farouk," Thor said in a low voice, "how has the questioning of the humans gone?"

He glanced at Vallah. "I'm not comfortable speaking in front of her."

"Why not?" she protested.

He slung his black braid over his shoulder and narrowed his eyes at her. "Because you're one of them. I don't trust you."

"Your commander asked you a question," Thor growled.

Farouk gritted his teeth. "There has been chatter of an escape plan. Some of the human men are holding some women in an undisclosed location. We're canvassing the area now."

I was right!

"Celebrate later, Halfling."

"I'll expect a bit more respect for my future wife, Farouk!" Thor was now leaning over Farouk, as if he were about to pummel him. "Any other information you've recovered, you'd better spit it out now. I haven't all day to waste on your mistrust of every living being on this planet!"

Future wife? What the absolute fuck? Vallah focused on her breathing. She was ready to dislocate both Farouk's knees if he didn't stop attacking her. What was with the future wife business? Thor said he'd like her to be his wife, sometime in the distant future but it wasn't if she had agreed. And Halfling? Technically, she was from the oldest Asgard family there was, according to Odin.

"I found two Centurion locator beacons in areas where some of the women have vanished. It appears they have beamed them aboard their ships."

"Fuck!" Vallah stomped away. She concentrated on the Centurions. What did she know about them? They were dying. They blended human DNA with their own. What did they want? They wanted...*Oh God, they want breeders.* She felt like vomiting.

It was then that the Asgard knowledge of the Centurions hit her fully. They wanted human women to make them babies, lots of babies, so that they didn't have to clone themselves. They'd messed around with their bodies so much they didn't know how to breed without technology? How was this possible?

But they wanted to wipe out the human race at the same time. But how would they breed without the humans, then?

Another memory hit her. The Centurions had visited Earth and planted the idea in the heads of state that women were property. Breeders. It was them, they did this to her people.

She was out for blood.

Thor gave Farouk a firm ass chewing about respect before firing him from his position.

Vallah followed him back to the café, meeting William behind the building. Thor demonstrated how the communication devices worked and how to find the code for each one. "There are more in storage when you run out. We are about to go to war, but if you go through the stargate with an Asgard, go to the main house and ask for Baldwin. He will know what to do."

William pulled his shoulders back. "Thank you, sir. But…when I get information, who do I give it to?"

He grabbed a red communicator, the only red communicator in the box. "This only has three buttons. The blue is for me. The red for Vallah. The green will reach someone else I trust. Share your information with only those three. Understood?"

William gave one firm nod, took the boxes, and walked away without saying another word.

"Let's head back. We need to prepare for our visitors. The Amazons and the Asgards are meeting soon. It's important that we are there." He began storming off.

"Thor? What's wrong?" She jogged a few paces to catch up.

"I dismissed your concerns, Vallah, your very accurate concerns, might I add. It's the same arrogance that has plagued our kind for generations. I should know better by now, but I'm angry at myself."

"Well you can stop being angry and just start listening." She elbowed him in the ribs.

It made him smile.

"I have a question." She chewed her lip, wondering if she really wanted the answer.

"Go on."

"Why did that fucknut call me a Halfling?"

He chuckled. "What's a fucknut?"

"A bad name. Why did he call me a Halfling?"

"He assumes you're part human since you came back with the others. We don't exactly go around disclosing the DNA of everyone, so no one has set him straight." His pace slowed. "I'm sorry about that. It was rude and uncalled for. Truth be told, I should have ended his

162

position long ago. But his father was a good man, and I guess I just expected him to be the same."

"And the future wife part?" Her voice lowered as she posed the question.

He shrugged. "Wishful thinking?"

Two marriage proposals since she landed on the new planet...she guessed she could be doing worse.

When they stepped through the stargate, they hurried to the meeting hall. It was packed full. The moment Thor walked in, everyone became quiet. It astonished Vallah how the Amazons respected his position.

Nadia approached him. "Commander, four of ours have come up missing. This is unprecedented. We do not stray, and an Amazon would never leave her post. But they are gone."

"When was the last anyone heard from them?"

"Before the last moon."

He put his hand on her shoulder. "And we shall draw the blood of every last Centurion until we find them."

"Blood will only be the beginning." She stepped back, allowing him to address the crowd.

"For the first time in centuries"—Thor began walking as he spoke loudly to the crowd— "our allies will band together to fight a common enemy. We will squash the vermin that have been a plague to our people. The Centurions cannot be allowed to continue killing and stealing their way through this system. It is up to us to bring them to an end."

The room erupted in a sound like *hua*.

"No longer are we going to sit back and take a passive approach!" he bellowed.

Hua.

"Blood will be spilled. Not all of us will make it back. But those that do will return victorious!"

Hua!

"And the halls of Valhalla will receive you with open arms."

Hua! Hua! Hua! The Asgards and the Amazons pounded on the tables.

"The delegations are set to arrive soon. The welcoming parties need to meet at the gate at the hour's end, ready to receive them. The rest are to prepare for battle. May the gods guide you and keep you safe!" Thor bowed his head and the room fell silent.

*

Why had he dismissed her convictions so easily? Vallah had been correct. So had the rest of the Asgards. It was humans *and* Centurions that were responsible for the human disappearances. The damned arrogance of the Asgards might be their undoing if they didn't learn to leave it behind.

Vallah's family was the only family trained by the Amazons. It was a deal made centuries ago. One that had purpose. With the Amazon training, an Asgard mentality, and a human upbringing...Vallah was a force to be reckoned with. But he'd dismissed her.

He'd not make that same mistake. She'd proven herself over and over again.

He kicked himself once more for intimidating her human friend, William. She was fond of him but displayed no emotion other than that. No other supreme commander in history was as ashamed as he in that moment.

But he'd made a valiant effort to right that wrong. The old ironsides would provide William with currency and some of the humans with a way to contact each other. Perhaps if the women could contact the men they wanted, they'd be less likely to fall victim to the Centurions again. Maybe they'd start fearing the Asgards less, too.

There was a lot of fear going on. The Asgards promised the humans they'd be safe—a promise they were failing to uphold.

Making love with Vallah, Seth, and Marika had given him hope for a large family. Vallah was so new to everything but was adjusting at light speed. Would she consider him as a husband? Would he finally have children of his own? He definitely needed a son or daughter to take his place as supreme commander one day.

He could imagine a little Vallah running around, full of fire and ready to take on the galaxy. With his stubborn streak and Vallah's tenacity, there would be no stopping their children. Marika was a softer and more loving woman. Her tenderness could give Vallah the comfort she'd been missing for so long.

Thor had to shake these thoughts out of his head. He was about to go into battle. There was no time for sappy thoughts of love and family.

CHAPTER FIFTEEN

Vallah dressed for battle, grabbing every weapon at her disposal. It didn't take long for her to realize that all of the Asgards wore a long cape. She was dressed as an Amazon. Out of place was what she was, but now was not the time for insecurity.

"I have something for you." Marika smiled as she approached. "This was my mother's." She held up an Asgard cape. "It looks like hide, but it's a micro woven material. It will deflect their energy weapons and keep you safe. Knives and projectiles can still penetrate it, so you're not invincible."

Vallah threw her arms around Marika. "If we make it out of this alive, I swear you'll never get rid of me. Thank you for everything." Her mother's cloak...what a sentimental gift.

"If?" She huffed. "You mean when." She winked at Vallah. "It's time."

They walked in threes to the stargate to head to the city. It took almost twenty minutes for them all to make it through to the other side. Not a word was spoken as they marched to the building holding the delegation. She really wanted to go with Thor to meet them all, but couldn't argue when he'd asked her to stay with the others. He had rank. She did not.

The allies began spilling out of the building upon their arrival. They joined them two by two. To Vallah's right was Marika and Tatiana. To her left was one Nyx woman and one Orithian man. The Nyx woman was tiny, maybe five feet tall. Her skin looked just as lavender in person as the photos she'd seen. The Orithian man was almost as tall as an Asgard, but twice as wide. His skin was bronze, like he spent most of his life in the sun. He had a staff weapon in his hand and all sorts of knives strapped to his body.

The Orithian queen stood at the head of the group. "The plan of attack has been explained to you all. The Nyx will do their level best to cloak you. Everyone else, Centurion is in season. Shoot and cut to kill. When we reach their high-ranking officials, we need them to remain living long enough to locate those they've taken. Then you may serve justice however you see fit. Elmhoard would like to say a few words."

Elmhoard's hair barely moved in the breeze. It reminded Vallah of purple cotton candy with sticks stuck in it. "The Nyx are masters of disguise. If you stay within four or five feet of a Nyx, the Centurions will never see you. Any further than that, then their bubble of protection will fade. We are prepared to die, but I do ask that you protect my people as we protect you. Each of you has been given one of these." He held up a small silver-looking device the size of a coin. "Should you find those on the battlefield injured and in need of care, place this on them and they will be beamed aboard an Orithian ship we have hidden in this sector. May the gods and goddesses protect and keep you."

Thor stepped front and center. "Brothers and sisters, Amazons, Nyx, and Orithians, I call on you now. Zeus himself watches over you as you march into battle. Let no Centurion man or woman stop you, and may you all come home safe. Amazon sisters, we have cherished your friendship since the beginning of time and, gods willing, we will call you sisters until the end of time. Now, we march!"

As they marched to the stargate, Vallah recalled the information that had been passed around. The Amazons insisted that three of them go first with bows and arrows. A Nyx man would hide them from sight as they stepped through the gate. They'd begin taking out whoever was in the way. It wouldn't take long for an alarm to be raised. They were all to walk through, assess, then pick up the pace.

Thor moved the stones and the gate came alive. Three Amazons stepped through. It was a few minutes before it was Vallah's turn. She took a deep breath. Marika gave her hand a squeeze. "We've got this."

Together, they stepped through. On the other side, it was dark...quiet. It was early morning and the gate had not been guarded. They made room for the others to step through. When the final warriors were on the planet, the gate closed.

Quietly, they marched toward the city. The dirt road beneath them was surrounded by grass. The land was nearly flat, which left for little cover. It reminded Vallah of the Civil War battles in the books she'd read.

"This is too easy," Marika whispered.

"It won't stay that way. Focus." Vallah looked around. Her insides felt queasy. It was at that moment she heard the whooshing of an arrow sailing through the air. Gurgling sounds followed. One of her Amazon sisters nailed the Centurion through the throat. It was only the first guard. They became more frequent as they made their way to the city center.

The Orithian man in her line began to break away. She wanted to call out to him, but they were to remain silent. What was he doing?

Vallah was forced to her right when the wind from an explosion pushed her—a bomb. It must have been what the Orithian was up to. It drew the Centurions out in hordes. The battle began almost instantaneously. She could see the city a few hundred yards in front of her. Their ranks dispersed as they fought with the Centurions.

She pulled her sword and ran at a man who had some sort of gun pointed at a Nyx woman. With one hard swipe, she nearly severed his arm. He began to scream again until she pulled her sword across his throat. The moment he dropped, another appeared behind him. She made quick work cutting the tendons in the backs of his legs.

She spotted Thor and Seth battling a group of ten all on their own. She took off at a dead run, cramming her sword in its sheath and pulling out two knives. As soon as she was in range, she took aim. While Seth was shielding himself with his cloak, the Centurion woman fired at him repeatedly. It was knocking him backward. Vallah released the knife. It soared through the air, nailing her in the side of the neck. She fell to the ground, holding her throat as blood poured out.

All of the training she'd received in her life could not have prepared her for the chaos, foul smells, and barrage of emotions soaring through her now. It was nearly impossible to tell enemy from ally. But Thor and Seth she could focus on. She turned to look behind her for Marika. They'd been next to each other when Vallah had taken off toward her two men.

Heat surged through her body, shooting from her back to her fingertips and toes as she was knocked off her feet. She'd been hit with something. Her muscles twitched, but she was able to get to her feet in time to see the Centurion with his gun aimed at her head. She rolled to the side and threw her second knife, landing it firmly in his eye socket.

Marika was on her heel. She held a gun of her own and began firing at a group of Centurions who approached. It fired red bursts of light at them. The ground under them erupted and they were thrown screaming into the air. "You okay?"

She stood over Vallah with her gun, guarding her until she was back on her feet. "That hurt like hell," Vallah complained as she drew her sword.

They continued to fight until they were in the city center. Vallah spotted the Orithian queen running toward a building. She was carrying a staff with a large blade at the top. In the windows of the building were humans pounding on the glass. The Orithian queen had found them.

"Thor!" Vallah screamed and pointed at the humans.

He nodded and fought his way toward the building. Vallah's foot hit something, and when she turned, she saw the bodies of a Nyx man, an Orithian woman, and...Tatiana, who was barely breathing.

"Keep moving," Tatiana choked.

She's alive!

Vallah reached in her belt pouch and pulled out a locator, slapping it on Tatiana's arm. "See you on the other side."

Tatiana glowed white before she disappeared.

Vallah looked around. The fighting was beginning to subside. Many bodies were strewn about the street, mostly Centurion.

She entered the building and listened.

"You can't have them!" It was Faith. "They don't belong to you!" She was standing at the top of the stairwell holding a large gun of some kind.

"Those Amazon women don't belong to you, either, human." It was the Orithian queen's voice.

Maybe Vallah could reach her sister. She stepped around the corner. "Faith? What are you doing? Do you even know?"

Faith's eyes widened at the sight of her sister. "I don't know you."

She took a few steps toward her sister. "Yes you do. It's Vallah. Now, do you want to tell me why you're kidnapping innocent women? Do you want them to suffer as you suffered?"

Her head twitched. Her lips curled as she bared her teeth. "What would you know about it? Who said they'd suffer, anyway?"

"You're surrounded, Faith. Most of the Centurions are dead or gone. Come down here and we can work this out. The Asgards understand that these have been trying times for us all." She kept her voice low. In her peripheral, she spotted a group of allies rounding the corner. "Put the gun down before you get hurt."

"Stay back! I have control!" Faith's face burned red as she screamed. "You can't have them back! You can't! It's my turn!"

My turn? My turn for what? It was clear that Faith's mind was twisted. What was also clear was that she had been integral in the kidnapping of the women.

Nadia looked to Vallah. With a heavy heart, Vallah nodded. Nadia drew back her bow and released an arrow that pierced Faith's hand.

Faith dropped the gun and screamed in pain, grabbing her bloody hand. When the allies rushed the stairs, her eyes connected with Vallah's before she pushed on a metal wrist cuff she wore. White light enveloped her, and then she was gone.

Vallah leaned against the wall, the air escaping her lungs. Though she had suspected her sister's involvement, she'd really hoped she was a victim and not the culprit. Salty tears stung her eyes.

Panic hit her in the chest as if she'd been shot with one of those Centurion energy weapons. She staggered back.

"Vallah?" Nadia ran to her side. "What is it?"

"I…I don't know."

Through the commotion of the victims being released, Seth pushed his way toward her. "Vallah!" When he reached her, he grabbed both of her arms. "It's Marika. They got her. She's alive, but…I don't know for how long."

"What do you mean, 'they got her'?" Her stomach hurt as if she'd been hit hard. Her chest began to ache and more tears stung her eyes. *Please be okay. Please.*

"They shot her in the face with their energy weapons. The synapses in her brain are firing like crazy and she was convulsing and—just come with me!" He grabbed her by the wrist and pulled her out of the building. Her heart thundered in her chest and her vision began to tunnel. Her best friend had been injured. She should have kept an eye on her, stayed with her. How could she have left her behind?

As soon as they were outside, he slapped a transmitter coin on her and the white light enveloped her.

CHAPTER SIXTEEN

When the light dissipated, Vallah found herself on the deck of what must have been the hidden Orithian ship. Many wounded were being cared for. The pungent odor of singed hair and burning flesh hit her first, then the cries of those in pain.

"The Valkyrie is on board. Please escort her to the medical wing." A large Orithian bronzed god stood to her left, directing those onboard. Vallah offered one firm nod and followed another Orithian woman who led her through the ship to Marika.

Her long, silky blonde hair was matted with blood and dirt. Though her eyes were closed, Vallah could see them whipping back and forth under her lids. Her muscles tensed and relaxed repeatedly. She lay in a chamber that reminded Vallah of the glass casket in her family's basement.

"We had to sedate her to give her body time to heal. The convulsions were fairly severe and violent. We've seen our kind recover from a shot to the head, but we don't know how the Asgard body holds up." The Orithian woman stood at Marika's feet. "She's a beautiful warrior. She fought valiantly. Be proud."

"I am. Thank you." She averted her eyes from Marika to the woman speaking. "I apologize; I didn't get your name."

She pushed the loose, dark tendrils from her face and pulled her shoulders back. "Lysippe. My brothers and sisters in arms call me Sip, as you may. It's an honor to meet you."

Vallah chuckled. "An honor? Really?"

Lysippe's eyes widened, displaying warm chocolate eyes behind her bronzed hard-ass exterior. "Vallah Sigrid of the Asgards, your plan of attack is the only reason the allies joined forces. It was smart. It was bold. Most of all, it was successful. Not one of the supreme commanders has brought us *all* together. Not in centuries."

"I wouldn't know." It was time for her to get back to her people. "Is she going to be okay?"

Lysippe looked at Marika, then at a monitor. "She is stable. Her brainwaves are all over the place, but that's to be expected until the energy dissipates from her body. She will likely be catatonic while her brain heals. I'm not the one in charge, and you should certainly have an Asgard physician make a diagnosis and prognosis. But from what I can tell, she will recover. The next few days might be touch and go."

"Can I get back down to the planet?"

She shook her head. "That's impossible. We are at hyper speed. We'll be arriving at your home planet shortly. The others have already gone through the gate, notwithstanding those that are transporting the bodies home."

Bodies. Just hearing that word made Vallah want to vomit.

"You're a Valkyrie now. It's customary for you to see—"

"The wounded and give them my appreciation. I remember." She did remember. Old instincts were surfacing, old information and customs…it was flooding back each day.

She made her way around to the wounded and thanked them for risking their hides. The few who were suffering gave her pause. She spotted an Asgard she recognized, but couldn't recall his name.

"Thank you for your bravery out there. Valhalla isn't ready to receive you just yet." She squeezed his hand.

"I must look pretty bad," he said with a laugh. "Maybe I should have had you teach me some of your knife skills."

"Baldwin?" The shock of realization hit her. Half his hair was gone, burned to the scalp. He was bleeding profusely from a wound in his leg that had been coarsely stitched together.

"Don't worry." He smiled. "The Asgard doc will have me back to my beautiful self in a day or so. We really need to share our medical technology with our allies." He coughed.

"We'll be back soon," she said, trying to reassure him. "I'm very sorry you were injured."

She tried to feel Marika but received nothing. Even walking by the medical pod didn't give her any indication of what her friend was feeling. She knew Seth was okay, but she hadn't yet seen Thor. Had he been injured?

"There you are," a voice croaked out. Vallah turned to find Tatiana lying on a bed, devices attached all over her body.

She wanted to cry. This fierce Amazon warrior had helped raise her, had taught her how to be not only a woman, but a warrior. She knew there was no way possible Tatiana would appreciate tears. It just wasn't the Amazon way. "How are you feeling?"

"Most of my ribs are broken, and a few of my organs were bleeding inside, but the Orithian medic is patching me up nicely." She lifted her sheet, displaying an abdomen full of deep purple-greenish wounds. "Think I can get Nadia to wait on me hand and foot?"

She couldn't help but chuckle, which felt like an odd

thing to do considering. "Doubtful. She'll have you training in the morning."

"Rest easy, child. We had a great victory today and our losses were at a minimum. You were valiant." She closed her eyes and began breathing heavily.

She let Tatiana sleep and moved into an empty room, watching the stars as they sailed through space. She spotted what had to be their planet, green and blue, off in the distance and stared out the window of the ship as they approached.

"Valkyrie?"

Queen Ayala stood with her arms crossed. Dirt and blood were splattered all over her.

"Queen Ayala, warmest greetings."

"No time for sentiments. This isn't over. Two of the women we rescued are pregnant with Centurion offspring. Your Amazons that were captured are pretty beat up. They'd been tortured for information."

"Jesus, they were raping them already?" Vallah's fists tightened.

"No, but the medical procedure was just as much of an intrusion. They were violated, impregnated against their will, and now the children they carry in their bellies are half theirs. Now they have to contend with that." The queen leaned against the wall, looking exhausted. Her shoulders slumped forward. "The worst part is, we could have avoided this. We knew what vermin they were and we did nothing because they weren't affecting the Orithians. So long as the Asgards and the humans were their targets, we turned a blind eye. That is not how one treats an ally. I will live with this shame for all of eternity."

Were queens usually this open?

"They're weakened by our attack. How long would it take to hit their home planet?" Vallah tasted blood and she wanted more. She wanted to crush them into oblivion.

"It's not that simple, Valkyrie."

"Vallah. Just…just Vallah. Why isn't it that simple? We

have the allies together. Everyone has to be just as pissed as we are. Let's go to their home planet and kick their ass."

Ayala grinned. "I knew I'd like you. You could be part Orithian." She forced herself off the wall. "The Centurions have a home planet, sure. But they've spread out and colonized many planets."

"So that's it, then?" Vallah felt like a deflated balloon. Her body felt heavy and sadness settled in.

She walked up to Vallah and put her hand first on her shoulder, then on her neck. "No, I still plan on attacking their planet, but this won't eradicate them completely." She pulled Vallah forward until their foreheads were touching. "And you're going to help me sell this idea to our leaders."

She pushed back slightly, putting an inch of distance between their faces. "Me? Fuck the gods, I'm not a commander or a queen. Why me?"

Ayala laughed and lightly smacked Vallah's face. "Because you are the Amazon-Warrior-Asgard-Valkyrie, and you're a goddamned genius. You have everyone's attention, and we're going to capitalize on that. But hear me, Valkyrie, the Orithians are with you, with our allies. We are angry and ashamed. I swear as queen; we will not fail our allies again."

She remembered sitting with William, sharing a meal. Her only concern then had been taking her sister back and getting back to safety. Now she was to conquer planets…races? *How did this happen?*

She and the queen stood in silence as they watched the planet's surface grow closer. When they finally touched down, the two made their way through the maze of hallways to the exit ramp. Vallah followed the crowd while in a daze. She needed food and rest, but how could she eat or sleep at a time like this?

Thor's voice snapped her out of her haze. "All Asgards and Amazons to the gate. Allies, to the black building down the street. Food and showers await your arrival." She wanted to run toward him, but kept her pace steady. When their eyes connected, she saw the look of relief wash over his face. So many emotions pelted her at once. She wanted blood, Centurion blood. The thought of food came and went. A shower sounded like heaven. Most of all, she was exhausted.

The humans had been returned, some of them running toward their temporary homes. The allies were trudging forward toward their accommodations as the Amazons and Asgards slowly made their way to the gate.

Finally, she reached Thor's side. Before she could say a word, he scooped her up in his arms, hugging her tighter than she'd ever been hugged. "Thank the gods you're okay. How is Marika?"

She shook her head. "She'll be out of it for a while. The Orithian woman told me it could take her awhile to come around."

"Not a chance. Our doctors will have her back to normal in no time. Let's go home." He put his arm around her and walked with her toward the gate.

"They're safe for now, Thor. But we should be waging an attack on their planet. Have a go at them while they're weak. They didn't expect us today. We need to keep that element of surprise...keep them off balance."

His laugh caused his shoulders to bounce.

"What?"

With a shake of his head, he chuckled as he spoke. "Are you sure it's not *my* father's DNA running through your veins? He said the exact thing to me only moments ago."

"Well I happen to like your father and respect his opinion." That wasn't true. She mildly liked him and only half respected him, but was sure that was about to change. Having someone force her to keep secrets had put her off. How could she blame a father for protecting his son?

When they stepped through the gate, the warm sunshine had been replaced by cool night air. "I'll never get used to that."

"The change in time?" he asked.

"Stepping through a wall of water that's not water and winding up somewhere completely different. It's really very…odd. It seems almost unreal. The change in time is just one aspect." With a deep breath of evening air, she shook her head. "How is it that I've only just arrived but feel like I've spent my entire existence here?"

He kept silent as they walked, affording her the opportunity to think aloud. She continued to talk about the planet, and how much of an improvement it was over what her life would have been on Earth. Before she realized it, they were at the main tree house.

"Thor, we should really hit them while they're down."

"What?" He shook his head, apparently deep in thought.

She rolled her eyes. "The Centurions—we should attack while they're weak and regrouping."

His head bobbed up and down. "We are also weak and regrouping."

"Commander Thor!" Queen Ayala came jogging behind them, two of her warriors in tow. "We need to talk."

"How did you find us?" he asked.

"Your Amazons led us most of the way. Can we talk?"

"Over dinner. I insist that we eat. We're all drained." He opened the door to the tree house.

"I would very much like to know how you Asgards blend with your environment," she said as she stepped through the door, "because this is spectacular."

As they stepped into the dining area, the smell of food reminded Vallah how hungry she really was. They took a seat and Freya began placing plates full in front of them.

"You should really have washed," she complained.

They ignored her complaints and dove into the meal, which reminded Vallah of pot roast. After several quick bites, the queen began to speak.

"We need to strike the Centurion home planet, and we need to do it while they're recouping. Our attack weakened their forces. I highly doubt they're prepared for another assault."

Thor's eyes darted from Vallah to the queen. The other two Orithians concentrated on their meal and nothing else.

"We have also suffered loss. Perhaps we should regroup as well." He placed his fork on the table. "Granted, our losses were not as great as theirs, but we have many wounded. The Nyx suffered the worst, as they had no combat skills."

"Negative, Commander! I think we should wage an air assault only. Clearly they've acquired Asgard beaming technology. I have no doubt you already realize you have a mole among your ranks. However, we don't need a lot of bodies, just ships. If we combine the Asgard fleet with ours, we can take out most of their ships, grounding them for an extended period of time. While they're grounded, we can continue to rid the outlying planets of the remaining Centurions until they understand that we will not tolerate them any longer."

Thor folded his hands and leaned back in his seat as he contemplated her proposal. "I will consider your proposal, if you'll consider mine."

Her left brow twitched. "I'm listening."

"The Orithian pilots and crew agree to be beamed aboard another ship if their ship is damaged beyond repair. I won't agree to anyone moving forward as a martyr. It's my only and final offer. Even if we all wind up on one ship to escape, I'll not tolerate any more senseless loss of life."

His words caused the queen's companions to cease chewing and stare at their queen.

"You want the Orithians to run?" the queen asked.

"No," Thor said, leaning forward, "I want you to order them to try to live. There's no need for them to die aboard a falling ship. Not when they don't have to. With more warriors of Orithia alive, they survive to fight another day, to end more Centurions, and to celebrate their victory in the great hall with their allies. After all, according to you, they'll be no match for us anyway. And if you and Vallah are wrong, and we do suffer the loss of many ships, the Asgards will work with you to replace your ships as swiftly as possible."

"Deal!" she shouted as she stood from her chair. "I will assemble my fleet. We'll meet outside your gravitational pull in two hours."

"Only two?" Thor laughed.

She smiled and gave a gentle nod. "You may be the supreme commander of the Asgards, Thor. But my ships and my warriors are mine to command. I sent for them prior to stepping through the gate. Don't worry, my second-in-command is already addressing Elmhoard so he doesn't feel left out, and your Amazons were ready to go before I said a word."

"The Amazons don't have ships," Thor chuckled.

"Of this, I am aware, but our cousins understand our position and offered any support we required." She turned to leave.

"Hold on," Vallah interrupted. "Can you use your scanners to find human life? They could have other humans."

"It was already on my mind. Rest assured, we'll save or *capture* any humans we find." He nodded. "Any objections?"

"None," Queen Ayala said before she walked out of the house.

"Vallah, shower and rest. I will come and get you as soon as we return." He put his hands on her arms.

"What? Absolutely not. I'm coming with you."

"No. You're not. You don't have the slightest idea how to fly a ship or fire our weapons. You will stay here. When we have time, I will get you up to speed on our technology. Until then, I'm the supreme commander, and I can't have someone with your lack of experience involved." He pulled her in and hugged her tight. "Please don't fight me on this. It's nothing against you. I need only pilots and helmsmen on this mission."

She relaxed and rested her forehead on his shoulder. "Come back safe." She couldn't argue with his logic. While she might have recalled some Asgard memories, flying was a learned skill. She wanted to see her mother and check on Marika.

Thor didn't need to be distracted by her presence or her questions. She had to find it within herself to be satisfied that the attack would happen. She had to trust her supreme commander and Queen Ayala for vengeance.

CHAPTER SEVENTEEN

She leaned on the side of the chair, trying to get comfortable while she watched Marika. She'd been taken out of the pod and placed on an Asgard healing bed. A laser continually traced her from the top of her head to her clavicle.

The doctor had told Vallah that she'd be awake in a matter of hours, but might be a bit twitchy for a few days. They really did have far superior medical advances. Why hadn't they shared them with their allies? To Vallah's implanted recognition, there was no reason not to share it. Was it just plain arrogance?

She had no idea how much time had passed as she dozed in and out.

"Vallah?" An Asgard woman stood at the entrance to Marika's room. "Commander Thor is on screen and he'd like to speak with you." She held her arm out, inviting Vallah to follow her.

They made it to a small room down the hall where Thor's image appeared on a glass panel on the wall.

"How is Marika holding up?" he asked with a smile. Smiles were good, it meant there was little to fret over.

"Doctor says she'll wake soon. How are things on that

end?" She tapped her foot, unable to contain her anxiety.

His head bobbed once. "We were victorious. The Orithians have about sixty very confused humans on board one of their vessels. There was a fleet of Centurion ships that had arrived moments before us. We were able to destroy them as well as the ships that were on the planet. We've seriously destabilized them for now."

"Is Faith...?"

He shook his head. "I'm sorry, Vallah. She wasn't on the planet, nor was she aboard the approaching vessels. We will keep searching for her."

"My mother...she isn't here. She mentioned an invitation from your father?"

A soft smile spread across his face. "They are good friends who are becoming reacquainted on Gefn. You can see her any time you like." Thor looked over his shoulder at his helmsman, who was speaking. "Looks like we will be back within the hour."

When the screen went dark, Vallah returned to Marika's room. She spoke to her sleeping friend, relaying the events that had taken place. "So the Centurions have had their asses firmly handed to them. The allies are bonding over victory. Yet here you are, lying around. You really need to open your eyes and let me know you're okay."

Marika mumbled.

Vallah's heart jumped.

"My head hurts." Her eyes opened and shifted from side to side.

"That's because you took a shot to the head with one of those energy weapons. You're safe now. The Centurions have been defeated." When Vallah saw one of the hospital staff walk by, she flagged them in. They began pushing fluids.

"Vallah can take you home in about ten minutes, Marika." The doctor smiled at her. "Your head is going to hurt for the remainder of the day. Just try to rest, and tomorrow you'll be a bit twitchy, but that will subside. Congratulations on your victory."

When the IV bag was empty, they let Vallah take Marika home. She was a bit shaky at first, but by the time they'd reached the gate, she moved with more grace, despite random muscle twitches.

"Damn, this feels awkward," she complained.

Vallah smiled and shook her head. "Well it looks strange as hell, if you were wondering."

Marika gave a solid laugh. "Very nice, Vallah." With a large grin and a roll of her eyes, she looped her arm in Vallah's and stepped through the gate.

On the other side of the planet, it was daybreak. Vallah and Marika were greeted by a group of Amazons, Orithians, and Asgards. Nearly thirty stood at the gate, cheering as they stepped through. Both women were hoisted into the air and marched to the hall.

They couldn't help but laugh and smile, Marika obviously doing all she could to hide the pain in her head. When they reached the hall, they were placed at the head table with eight other Asgard women, Thor standing behind them. Vallah wanted to turn around and throw her arms around him, but she sat instead. This was a ceremony…they'd earned their Valkyrie status.

"Our time-honored tradition of elevating an Asgard warrior woman to the rank of Valkyrie shall be honored here tonight. They've earned the right to adorn their bodies with the mark of the Valkyrie. The hawk, which has survived on every planet we've inhabited, will remain with them throughout all eternity. It is a sign of pride and honor. Please stand and show your respect for our fine warriors. I present the newest in the long line of Asgard Valkyrie to serve and protect the human race and their Asgard brothers and sisters."

The crowd began to scream, whistle, and cheer. Vallah stood with the others as her chest swelled with pride. She was one of them. More than that, she'd earned their respect.

When the cheering stopped, two tattoo artists approached the table and began laying the print of the hawk on the forearms of the newly anointed Valkyries. For a brief moment, anxiety flooded her. The old emotions about having her marked as fertile crept up, giving her pause. But this was her choice...a mark she'd earned by protecting the lives of others, for her ideas on saving the humans and decimating the enemy. The artist pulled his seat in front of her. After staring at him in the eyes for a brief moment and feeling nothing but pride coming off of him, she happily extended her arm.

The tattoo was placed with a painless laser. Within seconds, she was examining her arm, smiling at the hawk on her forearm. This was *her* mark. Hers.

"Congratulations, *Bella*." Seth slapped her shoulder as the warrior men did when they greeted each other. Before she could protest his use of Bella, he stepped around her and wrapped his arms around Marika.

Suddenly, the picture became clearer. Seth and Marika were more bonded, as Thor and Vallah had grown closer. Marika wanted more intimacy than just a friendship, she wanted a family. Sure, it was one that would share in pleasure, but it was more than that. It was a lifelong bond.

The thought of losing her had made her feel like something inside her was dying. She couldn't let that happen again. As much as she wanted to burst her feelings out loud, she had an idea.

She turned to Thor, who was shaking hands with the newest in his line of Valkyries. When he reached her, she threw her arms around his neck and pulled him in close. She whispered in his ear, "How about the four of us dine and retire tonight at your home? Is that okay?"

"As long as you're there, count me in." He gave her a quick kiss before moving on to the two women behind her that still needed congratulations from their supreme commander.

After things began to settle, Vallah insisted that Seth take Marika back to the tree house to get some rest. She then cornered Thor, suggesting they make their way out of the crowd. She waited as patiently as she could, glancing down at her new tattoo frequently. Any feelings of unease she had about it had vanished. She was like a new bride showing off her wedding rings.

She watched Thor, his dark ponytail swaying as he moved. His broad shoulders bouncing as he chuckled. Eyes blue as the ocean creasing at the sides as he smiled. His strong jaw covered in stubble from a few days of growth.

Finally, after making his rounds, they were able to duck out of the hall and headed toward his home hand in hand.

Thor gave her a play by play of the battle that had ensued at the Centurion home planet, and she updated him on their injured friends. When they reached his home, they sprawled on the bed. Fatigue hit Vallah hard the moment her body became relaxed.

"Thor, I want to know exactly what you want from a family."

He leaned up on his elbow and looked down on her. "As long as you're in the picture, I'm flexible."

She rolled her eyes. "That's easy to say now, but I'm talking forever here. I'd like to know what you want."

He leaned in and kissed the tip of her nose.

"Hey, I'm a fierce Valkyrie now. No nose kisses!" She laughed and nudged him with her shoulder. "I'm serious, now get serious too!"

After a deep sigh, he rolled to his back and stared at the ceiling. "After my wife died, I never thought I'd ever marry again. I thought of our marriage as perfection in every way. But that was my marriage to her. I want children. I wish to make you Vallah Westergaard, if you'll take my surname. You may wish to keep Sigrid, and I'll have no objections. But my wish is for you to take my name and let me make you mine."

"And having others in our marriage?" She chewed her lip nervously waiting for his response.

"You're thinking of Seth and Marika?"

"Does that bother you?"

He laughed. "Seth and I have been friends since we were very young. Admittedly, I did feel a bit jealous when I realized you two had a relationship. That has subsided, because I can see you're more drawn toward me, and as selfish as it may be, I like it that way. He seems more drawn to Marika, so no one is left alone. But what about you? Are you comfortable with such a marriage? I know the humans didn't believe in such arrangements."

"Actually, some cultures did. I read about it in one of the many, many historical books the Amazons forced me to read. Polygamous relationships weren't the norm, but they did exist in some areas. It's just...I never thought of myself having a lasting relationship, let alone a marriage. A marriage of four was admittedly a foreign idea when Marika mentioned it. But now, anything else seems absurd."

He rolled toward her again, grabbed her by the shoulder, and turned her to face him. "That arrangement would make me very happy. And if you wish it, we can propose it tonight."

She smiled and nodded. "That would make me happy too."

In an instant, his lips crushed hers. She pulled him closer, reveling in the affection. His tongue teased her lips briefly before he finally sat up, smiling. "You've made me the happiest man in the universe."

"We're going to need a bigger house." She laughed. "Your bed is in your living room."

"Whatever you wish, the forest will provide."

She shook her head. "Oh no. I love this place. We just might have to add a big bedroom or something. And a bigger bed."

"As you wish." Gently, he pushed her on her back,

tucked his fingers in her pants, and pulled them to her knees. He took his time removing her boots and tunic. She watched as his eyes traced her body as he removed her clothes.

When her top finally came off, he sat back and admired her body. "You are one stunning creature." He wasted no time disrobing himself before he kissed his way up her legs, to her stomach. He lingered at her breasts, savoring each nipple, gently squeezing her flesh. "With amazing breasts that I could enjoy all day."

She giggled as he gave them one final nip and worked his way up to her neck. Gentle kisses and licks had goosebumps rising all over her body.

He whispered in her ear, "I can't believe I get to enjoy you for the rest of my life."

Needing sleep but feeling needy, she couldn't wait for the foreplay. She reached down and grabbed his hard dick, stroking it, mimicking him. "I can't believe I get to enjoy *you* for the rest of *my* life. Now don't make me wait any longer."

He obliged, pushing the head into her entrance. He paused, taking a deep breath. As he began to push into her again, she felt every inch of him. Her body welcomed him and her skin was set ablaze. His tongue grazed her lips once more and her breathing hitched. Thor had a way of setting every nerve on fire. With a hand tangled in his hair, she pulled him in for the kiss that hovered just above her lips. She wanted all of him, in her mouth, in her pussy.

His thrust caused her to moan into the kiss. She could feel the smile on his lips and knew he enjoyed causing the noises she made. She released his hair and let her hands slide down to his strong shoulders. She could feel the muscles rippling under her fingers as he moved above her. He was strong, sexy, and an excellent lover.

The sex with Thor and Seth had been mind-blowing, but this time—this time he was making love to her. She could feel the emotion rolling off of him. It felt warm, comforting, and all-encompassing. His hands slid down to her thighs, and he pulled them up over his hips. Then he scooped his hands under her shoulders and lifted her so she was sitting on him.

He hugged her tight as he pumped into her from below. Devouring her lips once more, he squeezed her shoulders. She couldn't breathe, not that she cared. She held on firmly, tossing her head back and gasping for air. Sweet pressure began to build low in her belly. Her hands began to tingle as an explosion of color clouded her vision.

Once again, her orgasm was his undoing. He groaned out his own release and held on to her, resting his forehead on her sternum.

"I love you, Vallah," he gasped out.

She kissed the top of his head and hugged him tight. "I love you, Thor." It had finally hit her what love was, and she had it. She had it with him. She had it with Marika. She might eventually have it with Seth, once she let go of old hard feelings.

They collapsed on the bed. Post-coital bliss sedated them into a deep slumber.

****

Thor and Vallah had prepared the meal together. While a lot of their meat came from animals that were foreign to her, she finally had a steak the way she liked it, medium-rare. The rest of the table was set with fruit, sautéed vegetables, rolls, salad, and potatoes. Thor had rushed into the city and retrieved a few bottles of aged wine that had been gifted to them by the Orithians, who were apparently expert wine makers, or oenologists, as Thor had called them.

With Seth and Marika joining them at the table, the four ate and drank wine. Spirits were high with the victory, as well as from Marika and Vallah elevating to Valkyrie, and most of the Asgards returning home safe.

"How's your head?" Vallah asked.

"The doctor was right. After taking another nap and drinking about three liters of water, I feel almost perfect." She chewed another piece of steak. "Okay, I definitely want more of this in the future. Who knew beef would taste so good? Cows seem so lazy."

Vallah laughed and shook her head. It was good to see her friend laugh. She now wanted to increase her happiness. "I asked you two over tonight because I, well, *we* have a proposition." The pace of her heartbeat quickened. She laced her fingers in Thor's for support.

"Not another war!" Marika's shoulder's fell. "I need a day off!"

Thor laughed. "No imminent threats so far."

Seth's eyes darted back and forth between Vallah and Thor. "This is going to be a doozy. I can feel the anticipation in you both."

"Don't spoil this, idiot. We're asking you two to marry us."

Seth dropped his fork. "What?"

Marika shot out of her chair and squealed. "Really?"

"I'm sorry. What?" Seth repeated.

Vallah narrowed her eyes at him. "Am I that objectionable?"

He shook his head and squinted his eyes. "You're adorable. But I have to be married to *him*?"

Thor beamed him in the head with a roll. "I'm pretty good-looking. Who are you kidding?" he teased.

Vallah couldn't help but laugh at the two of them.

Marika picked up her roll and threw it at Thor. "Stop it, you two! This is huge! Seth...I want this. Do you want us?"

"Sure. I guess I can be married to the supreme commander. Does this come with extra benefits?" He ducked before he could get assaulted by any more baked goods. After they resumed their seats and eating their meal, Seth finally had a serious look on his face. "So I guess this means I have been forgiven?"

Vallah placed her fork on the table and leaned in. "I understand why you had to deceive me. Absolution might take a bit longer, but I no longer hold it against you. Odin helped me to understand our ways and our unwritten laws in the short time we visited him. It's important for us to protect our brothers and sisters. I shouldn't have expected you to disobey your supreme commander. I just didn't understand what that meant at the time. That will have to be good enough for now."

"You not hating me is good enough for me." He grabbed Marika's hand. "We're going to be married."

"We didn't…I mean, I didn't…what about children?" The hopeful look in her eyes could have brought down the strongest of men.

"I'd love children," Seth said with a smile.

"Me too," Vallah agreed.

Thor squeezed Vallah's thigh. "I've always wanted children. I can't imagine any group other than those sitting at this table better suited to raising them."

"There's one thing I need to understand, and you'll excuse me if it's awkward. But…there's still some details I need ironed out." Vallah needed to put her anxieties to rest.

"All you need to do is ask. Everyone here understands who you are, Vallah, and we know we will have to fill in the holes for you. There's no need to be shy or ashamed." Marika lifted her glass. "You already know I blurt everything anyway."

"How do we decide who has whose children?"

Marika set her glass down and looked at the others at the table. "Oh…that."

The silence was killing her. "Isn't there a rule of thumb or something?"

"I don't get the question," Seth finally said.

Marika rolled her eyes. "You can really be thick sometimes. She's asking if I'm having your babies and

Thor's babies and vice versa."

Seth shrugged his shoulders. "Oh. I don't know. Do we draw a short stick or something?"

Marika finally slugged him in the shoulder. "You should stop talking."

"I think we live as a family for a short time, and then decide what works best for us. I think every family dynamic is unique. We all agree we do nothing until it is discussed and agreed on by all."

"Wait, it's not...I just...I want children. I'm just not ready to start doing that quite yet. And I don't know how I feel about having Seth's children."

Marika leaned in. "You don't object to me carrying Thor's seed, though?"

"Heavens, no. You'll be a fantastic mother!"

She released a breath and collapsed in her chair. "Oh. Oh, wow. Okay. I thought for a minute I was the problem."

Thor laughed. "I thought *I* was the problem."

"Nope. Just me." Seth folded his arms over his chest. "What's wrong with my genetics?"

Vallah chewed her lip. "Odin showed me something...we are, uh...we're cousins. Distant cousins, mind you. But I don't know if that causes a problem. Humans found it to be an issue in ancient times. They called in inbreeding. Royalty would often inbreed on purpose for a pure bloodline, but then they discovered the babies of close relations had issues. I just...I'm concerned if our DNA is too closely matched. I just want healthy children, Seth. That's all."

Thor put his arm around her. "You will be fine. You're not closely related, and we rarely have any issues with our children. We're good stock."

Relieved and seeing no issues moving forward, Vallah stood and raised her glass. "To my new family."

The other three raised their glasses.

This was it. She was going to be married to three other

people. She'd gone from a lonely orphan to this. She belonged to someone. She belonged to three someones.

THE END

ABOUT THE AUTHOR

Anita Cox is a bestselling author of a growing number of novels. For over ten years, she's written contemporary, erotic, and paranormal, romances via traditional, independent, and audio publishers.

An only child born and raised in the Midwest, Anita enjoyed reading novels as a way to occupy herself and set her imagination free. That propensity blossomed into creations of her own as she began crafting novels of her own. As she matured, she began writing more adult tales and donned the penname Anita Cox.

Anita resides in Indiana with the last teenager in her herd, a fluffy-not-fat cat named Tommy Chong, Titan the English Mastiff and the husband that helped create her creative penname. In her free time, Anita enjoys fishing, gardening, and devouring equal portions of strong coffee and well-written novels.

BOOKS BY ANITA COX

SHIFTER CHRONICLES

Pursuing Grace
Saving Grace
Resurrection
No Quarter

TALES OF THE ASGARD

Valkyrie

DIRTY WHITE CANDY

The Beginning
Ultimate Vacation
Trading Places

www.ingramcontent.com/pod-product-compliance
Lightning Source LLC
Chambersburg PA
CBHW060809120626
46557CB00001B/141